# UNMASKING A MARRIAGE

# Unmasking a Marriage

PATRICIA MAY

Clear Mind Press

# Contents

# Legal page

Unmasking a Marriage
Patricia May
April 2023

Images on cover: Ben Mack

ISBN Ebook: 9780645707458
ISBN Print: 9780645707441

Clear Mind Press, Australia
Copyright © Patricia May
Legal deposit in the National Library of Australia
Design and layout interior: Clear Mind Press
Clear Mind Press: www.clearmindpress.com
Cover Design: Clear Mind Press

DISCLAIMER: People, places and perceptions have informed and inspired this work of fiction. However, the story, all names, characters, and incidents depicted in this production are fictitious. No identification with actual persons (living or deceased), places, buildings, and products is intended or should be inferred.

# Chapter 1

Thursday morning.

"Hey Andy! You awake?" Bang, bang, bang! "C'mon ya lazy bastard. Wake up!" The fierce hammering on the back door and the boisterous barking of his two kelpies jolts Andy reluctantly into consciousness. The bedside clock is blinking at quadruple zeroes. Power's been off. Rummaging around the base of his bed, he finds yesterday's tracky-dacks, and takes several precarious attempts to manoeuvre his feet into separate leg holes before staggering down the hallway, ricocheting off the walls to the kitchen. In a pantomimic finale, he knocks over a chair as he stumbles to a halt against the back door. One hand holds up his pants, the other holds the flyscreen door firmly shut. Through blearily blinking eyes, he sees Jim Kessel, his aged farming neighbour, standing impatiently before him, making no attempt to conceal his irritation and contempt.

"Rachel called. She says ya haven't answered ya phone. Sal comes outta hospital today. Ya meant ta be pickin' her up!"

"What time is it?" Andy glides a palm over his balding head, his thumb and forefinger sliding bewilderingly to rub sleep from his eyes. "What's today?" he croaks.

"It's nine 'o' bloody clock! Thursday! October twenty bloody nine! Jesus mate. Ya need ta get off the piss. It's doin' ya brain in. An' I bet the house's a bloody mess." Jim attempts to pull the flyscreen door open, leaning to one side as he peers in. Andy pulls it shut; the sudden movement and loud slam setting the dogs off again.

"And I'm lettin' these poor little bastards off their chains. Ya wanna live in ya own shit, okay. But ya shouldn't be makin' them live in theirs." The dogs bounce off the verandah to lap frantically at the water in the fishpond before scurrying through the side gate into the paddock to relieve bladders and bowels.

"Right," grunts Jim. "I can see you're in no bloody state to make a decision! I'll phone the hospital; get Rachel ta tell Sal ta catch the midday bus an' get off at the pub. And you can clean ya self up. Maybe even try clearing that bloody shithole ya think I can't see. You're a bloody disgrace. Ya need a bloody good boot up the arse!"

This violent awakening foreshadows the shift that will see Andy's world implode. He holds the screen door closed, waiting for the side gate to slam shut confirming that Jim has gone, and turns to hazily consider the chaos that has accrued these past two weeks. The sink and benches are littered with dirty dishes and he fleetingly regrets his petulance in refusing to learn how to use the dishwasher. Sally's biscuit and cake tins clutter the kitchen table, their desiccated left-over contents now being methodically hijacked by a legion of tiny sugar ants. A yellow pool of butter floats in its dish, stale bread spewing out of the plastic bag next to it. A confusion of sauce bottles and jam jars are missing their lids, and a discarded baked bean tin stuffed with used teabags rests next to the wilted remains of a roast leg of lamb haphazardly abandoned on the table. Dominating the domestic debris is a large, overfilled ashtray surrounded by a confusion of rollie cigarette paraphernalia and empty beer cans.

A couple of cartons filled with more empty beer cans and rum bottles sit next to the overflowing kitchen bin, its flip-top lid missing amongst the mess. Several blow flies and a cloud of their smaller bush buddies cruise around this kitchen carnage, casually sampling the mouldering morsels clinging to dishes, cans and wrappers. The bench next to the phone is littered with unopened mail and consignment notes, left over crate labels, several short lengths of wire used to prise beetles from blocked irrigation sprinklers, and other miscellanea pulled from his pockets. A tirelessly blinking red light on the answering machine signals messages he hasn't bothered to listen to.

He shuffles out to the toilet in the farm's laundry bathroom on one end of the verandah. Letting his track pants slide to the floor as he steadies himself with a hand against the wall, he relaxes into a long, loud, and malodourous piss. Discarded work clothes rest in a dishevelled heap around him. He bends unsteadily to retrieve his pants, and is startled by an unsolicited fart liberated by the effort. It kickstarts his brain, waking him sufficiently to surrender to the day. There are things to be done. He's not sure what, except that Sally features at the end of it.

The dogs haven't returned, enabling twenty or so chickens to resume unchallenged, their attack on Sally's large vegie garden. They scratch and peck at her seedlings, scattering compost litter and their droppings over the concrete pathways. The chook house door is wide open, pellet feeder and water dispenser empty, nests overflowing with eggs. On the verandah a determined trail of meat ants circumvents the dogs' soiled bedding, intent on gathering the crusty crumbs clinging to bowls and discarded empty food tins. Andy raises both hands to his head as his muddled mind gradually assesses the mess he is in.

He is now overwhelmingly aware of the smell of fermenting tomatoes too ripe for market or local sale, mingling with the classic pong of putrid seed potatoes, all rotting in their crates in the car port. Sundry bags of chicken manure have been left sagging against the fence and collapsing bags of sheep dung are spilling out of the trailer parked nearby. He promised Sal a month ago that he would empty it all into the compost pit.

Gotta have a drink. There's none in the fridge. Lifting and shaking empty beer cans, he finds one opened and almost full. He sucks on it greedily, belches long and loudly, and slams the empty down onto the table. Fumbling frustratedly with a fragile cigarette paper, his trembling fingers unable to assemble a line of tobacco, he searches in desperation to find half a butt in the ashtray. He blows the ash dust from it and lights it, twisting his head to one side to avoid singeing his nose hairs as he inhales deeply. The warm stale beer and nicotine cocktail immediately hijack the battle raging between his head and his guts. He staggers urgently to the kitchen bench and vomits forcefully into the sink.

An hour or so later, two hastily filled plastic rubbish bags sit atop the crates of rotting tomatoes in a juvenile attempt to conceal them, while the fetid smell of their escalating putrefaction remains. Four cartons of empty beer cans and several empty rum bottles sit in the back of the ute, destined to be anonymously abandoned next to the roadside bins at the truck stop on his way to town. Jim's reference to this latest alcoholic binge has prompted this attempt to eliminate the evidence.

Garbage removed, he endeavours to tidy the kitchen, stacking the cake tins, returning lidless jars to the pantry and rinsing away the remnants of his earlier retching before confining the dirty dishes to a more structured arrangement in and about the sink. He sweeps the floor; clumsily urging the kitchen chairs back into place under the table. Lacking the domestically informed perspective that comes from long-standing practice, he neglects to wipe away crumbs and spills from the table and benches or replace the bin liner.

His stomach has settled but is not yet ready for food. He'll get something at the pub while he waits for Sal. Standing wearily under the steaming shower, comforted by the stream of hot water hammering the top of his head and cascading down his back, stilling his panic and tempering his emotions, he finds himself contemplating her return. Her absence, unexpected, unprepared for, has rudely dislocated his life.

She has been a constant presence since she moved in with him and his mother. For those early married years, he had two women under the same roof meeting his every need except one, his carnal comforts satisfied elsewhere. Sally has never showed any interest in sex, her celibacy being a condition of their marriage, initially supported by her advancing pregnancy. She had been completely focussed on her twin boys' care and wellbeing thereafter. He'd never hidden the fact that he was pursuing a sex life away from home. Indeed, his mother had insisted on it, her only condition being, that he be discreet and not bring shame on the family.

But he's had no inkling as to how much his Sal has been the glue holding his life together. Her daily routines, her dutiful management of his every domestic need, providing the invisible structures, the continuity and security enabling him to give his best efforts to their mixed farming business. How did it all collapse around him so quickly? He just wants his life back.

* * *

Thursday morning.

"You won't know yourself Sal." Rachel gently releases the last of the sutures. "You look ten years younger. The colour is back in your cheeks and some life back in your eyes. Time away from Andy has wiped that worn-down weariness from your face." Sally says nothing and feels nothing, other than the minor discomfort of this final procedure.

Sorry," Rachel attempts to qualify herself, "He's my cousin. I know him, and he's always been an angry little shit. He's a bully and a smart arse. How do you think he earned the title Andy the Arsehole?" She whips off her latex gloves, flicking them into the dressing tray before deftly wrapping the surgical debris into a neat blue plastic parcel. She drops it purposefully into the heavy-duty rubbish bag pegged to the side of her trolley.

"He should have had a good boot up the arse when he was five, Uncle Jim says." She grins and rolls both the trolley and her ample buttocks towards the door. "I'll just get the discharge paperwork sorted and then call you a taxi. The doctor says you're good to go."

Sally smiles resignedly. Nurses, like teachers who marry farmers, inevitably return to work; conserving the viability of family properties while clinging to their separate identities and independence. Chances are that you'll always know someone on the nursing staff at this regional hospital. Rachel is family; sort of. The daughter of Andy's mother's cousin. They meet infrequently at weddings and funerals, bump into each other at the post office, and attend community gatherings where a show of interest or support is mandatory. Rachel is a confident, caring, and competent nurse. She is also never short of an opinion.

Despite the functional yet comfortable austerity of the room, Sally is sorry to be leaving; physically but not emotionally ready to relinquish the sanctuary this unexceptional space has afforded her. Despite her surgery, preceded by a week of preparatory rest and blood transfusions, she feels she has been on a retreat, separated from her day-to-day world and the unwieldy weight of it. Her hysterectomy had been scheduled following a last resort consultation with a doctor she had selected from the yellow pages; and this only when her bleeding days outnumbered her dry; with the breathlessness that accompanied any exertion intruding on her daily routines. She had expected the surgery with a resigned sense of relief, the conclusion of an increasing physical debilitation. It had been a covert arrangement, meticulously planned and prepared for, with her informing Andy only the day before her admission to hospital, his response erupting exactly as she had expected.

"Whad-a-ya mean ya goin' ta hospital. What for? An' who says? What am I supposed ta bloody do?"

"Yeah. Yeah. There's food in the bloody fridge 'n' freezer, an' yes, I know where the pantry is. What about the fuckin' orders? Who's printin' the bloody labels?"

"Oh Mrs Fuckin' Smarty Pants. Always got a fuckin' answer. You an' ya fuckin' lists. Course I know how ta write an invoice. I'm not a fuckin' idiot."

"Ya coulda told me before. Let me at least have some notice. This is fuckin' bullshit." He had slammed the back door belligerently, striding cantankerously to his ute to drive to the pub; the habitual salve and solution to any and all of life's daily frustrations. He has neither visited nor left her messages while she has been in hospital, for which she is truly grateful, suspecting that Rachel has kept him suitably informed to ensure he kept his distance.

She gazes one last time at her reflection in the bathroom mirror. Her pastel floral blouse hangs loosely from her shoulders, tucked into tailored linen trousers. She has long taken pleasure in sewing her own clothes but never been motivated to explore the more sophisticated fashion trends, clinging to a safe, conservative style. Running a brush through her hair she deftly manipulates it into a loose plait resting low on the back of her neck, the simple grooming solution she has long chosen over dependence on a hairdresser. And, like so many of her choices, offering no impetus or challenges that might push Andy's irritability buttons. A quiet life at any cost. She rarely wears make up, but today, on a whim, reaches into her toilet bag in search of a lipstick. Finding none she decides to buy one.

The taxi driver greets her with a nod. He'd received instructions on her destination with the booking. His respectful silence is both a comfort and a consolation. She is in no mood for idle chatter, still basking in the guilt-free inertia that her surgery allowed her, wallowing in comparative luxury. This included the measured pleasure she took in choosing each of her meals from the menu delivered with the breakfast tray. Morning and afternoon tea had been offered discreetly, its arrival heralded by the intermittent rattling of the trolley meandering around the corridors; the pink lady respecting her wish for solitude and privacy as suggested by partly drawn curtains and her quiet demeanour.

Once detached from the drip and catheter, she had casually celebrated her freedom walks via the lift to the café where she could buy an espresso coffee and flip through the junk magazines; or watch the birds at play in the paved garden area as they scavenged for insects and crumbs. The gentle afterglow of this newfound self-indulgent slothfulness, and a growing sense of liberation, travels with her during her taxi ride to the bus station.

Intent on avoiding the curiosity of acquaintances, she chooses not to sit waiting for the hour before her bus departs, but stows her overnight bag in a locker and strolls aimlessly around the shops in the mall, stopping at the ATM to withdraw two hundred dollars; wondering as she does so what she will do with it. She so rarely uses cash, nor has the need for it. She is celebratedly bemused by the feeling of decadence in having paper money sitting in her wallet alongside the assorted plastic cards that confirm her identity, authorise purchases and acknowledge her memberships to sundry organisations and services. Most of them have barely been used in recent months. Her diminishing health and unexpected flooding compromising her movements any distance from home.

She is untempted by any of the eateries and unready for the social interactions these might incur, but impulsively purchases a new pair of jeans, a checked shirt and a pair of runners, immersing herself in the carefree extension of her emerging indulgence in private pleasures. Intent on avoiding them being seen and questioned by Andy, these uncharacteristically frivolous purchases are packed alongside her nighties and toiletries in her overnight bag. She is fleetingly hopeful he has recovered from his grand sense of woundedness. Perhaps even just a little pleased to see her, outside of the relief in having his housekeeper and business manager back.

By choosing the front seat behind the bus driver, she has a clear view of the highway, instinctively needing to see the road ahead. There is no-one she knows on board and the dozen or so co-passengers look to be backpackers or itinerant workers on their way to seasonal farm work further south. How long has it been since she last travelled by bus? When not her own driver, which is almost all the time, she is a reluctant passenger with Andy on the rare occasions when they attend a function together. Mostly the end of season piss-ups for the football or axeman's clubs where a showing of the missus is mandatory. Andy has travelled with her but once to an assembly at the boys' boarding school in the city, and never a parent's night; always finding a more important engagement; but mostly just not bothered to get home from the pub in time to make the two-hour journey. She believes it is more about his disregard and contempt for scholastic domains.

Her twin boys, now emerging into manhood, are in their final term of year eleven and rapidly separating themselves from home and the backwater they feel they've grown up in. The choice to send them away when they reached high school age, was made when they were just entering primary school. It was then that a trust fund was set up specifically for their education, with both Margaret, her mother-in-law, and her parents contributing. Sally too had deposited surplus cash when cattle prices and cash crop returns allowed, as well her inheritance when her parents died. Her primary intention has ever been to secure her boy's future.

Neither of her parents had had any respect or affection for Andy. Both had died prematurely, her father from a sudden fatal heart attack at forty eight, as he lifted the outboard motor from his fishing dinghy; and her mother from the untreated leukaemia she'd kept secret from them all just twelve months later. Her boys have only misty memories of their maternal grandparents.

They had enthusiastically embraced the move away. Home had been heavy with the uncertainties surrounding their persistently irritable and belligerent father, the obvious and accelerating disaffection between their parents, and the intrusion that living with their disabled paternal grandmother had on their lives. Nanna Chester, Margaret, had always been there, but rendered semi paralysed and almost speechless by a stroke when they were eight years old and attending the local primary school; the very same one that Sally and their father had attended years before. Margaret died in her sleep three years ago. Andy's impatience, irritability and belligerence has escalated exponentially since then.

The move to boarding school has enriched their growing attachment to Sally's brother and his long-term partner. Uncle Brian and Aunty Millie, aka Milton, are family to the boys; their buffers and trusted confidantes when their father's boorish and egocentric behaviours annoy them. Andy, of course, has zero tolerance for 'Fuckin poofters!'

Free of the distractions or the discipline of driving, Sally finds herself seeing so much more from her majestically elevated position in the bus. She is reminded of her school bus years nearly two decades earlier and is surprised by the emotional echoes of the past as old icons are recognised or their absence noticed. Chooky Fowler's driveway and his milk can letterbox are still in place but only the fruit trees that had skirted his house remain. The seedlings that were planted along road verges by her primary school class one Arbor Day now cast broad shadows across the highway.

There is both a mild excitement and a soothing comfort in the way the bus cruises confidently along the road, the hum of its diesel engine competing companionably with the gentle cooling breeze of the air conditioner. She feels completely at ease, relieved in fact, to have an anonymous and obviously capable driver to take her home. This prolonged release from responsibility and the gentle oscillations of the bus traversing the highway are having a wonderfully analgesic effect, not that dissimilar to her pre-surgery medication before the magical release of the anaesthetic. And hours later the post-operative pethidine, pacifying her pain, leaving her drifting in and out of slumber.

There had been no decisions to be made. She had been gently guided or instructed when and where to move; her feet and legs massaged, and drinks and food proffered before she recognised her need for either. Pillows had been plumped, the TV angled, and the personal controls explained as they were placed within easy reach. Curtains and blinds adjusted just so and strong caring arms preparing and steadying her for her first post-operative shower. She had been discovered quietly weeping and it was thought she was grieving the loss of her womb, her womanhood.

She'd been unable to explain that it was the overwhelming sense of humility and gratitude for the care, kindness and comfort she was receiving. It had been so long since she had been offered or felt worthy of such intimate attention.

Reality returns as the bus slows to town speed, the bridge over the river looming, the pub less than a minute away. She reaches for her bag and begins readying herself for her reunion with Andy, resignation replacing the dread that has risen fleetingly in her stomach. Air brakes hiss as the bus glides gently to a halt and the door opens.

Andy's work ute is parked in its usual place. He is standing on the pub verandah, a beer in one hand and a rollie cigarette in the other, leaning up against the windowsill as he talks to two of his mates. Smokers, most of the regulars in this pub, are now forced to feed their addictions outdoors. She recognises the wily father and son who abandoned their mixed orchard to start a free-range egg and chicken enterprise.

The old man continues talking, oblivious to the bus having just pulled in. Only Andy looks straight across at Sally. He gives no indication that he has seen her; in fact, just watches her blankly, listening to his mate, and making not the slightest flicker of acknowledgment. Becoming aware of the thrum of the idling diesel engine, the old man stops speaking and both he and his son turn to follow Andy's gaze. Sally looks at all three of them, standing there in their work-stained clothes, staring back at her with disinterest. Flicking his cigarette to the ground, crushing it with his boot as he lowers his glass, Andy now looks directly at her, expecting her to step down and walk towards him. She stares back. Frozen. Emotionless.

"You getting off love?" The driver turns to Sally, standing stock-still, bag in hand, glued to the top step. Startled out of her paralysis she turns to him and stammers, "I'm sorry.......I...... I've changed my mind. Let me off around the corner at the bus stop opposite the church."

"Sure thing." The door glides shut.

She is relieved to see no-one, checking both ways before crossing the highway and walking purposefully to the porch of the Anglican church. She rests her bag on the wooden bench and lowers herself gently next to it, breathing rhythmically as she relaxes into her surrounds, reminded by the familiar musty smells that this is a safe place. The church is well known to her despite having ceased any religious affiliations long ago. It is where she was baptised and then confirmed, infrequently attending Sunday School as a child and for a short time sitting obediently amongst the meagre customary congregation in her mid-teens. She had accompanied her girlfriend and her family while her own parents sat at home in discrete bewilderment at her pretend piety. Her boys had been baptised here, but she and Andy had not had a church wedding. In fact, they'd had no wedding at all, just driving to the city with bulging belly to marry in the Registry Office. Up and back in a day, returning to live with Andy's mum, on the farm, where she has been ever since.

"Ah Sal. How nice to see you. Stand and let me give you a hug. It's been too long." Stanley, the long-time pastor, lowers his wheelbarrow and removes his gardening gloves. They embrace with genuine affection. He is recognised as the comfortably gay Anglican minister. He lives alone with Emma, his Labrador dog, in their quaint little manse surrounded by a disorderly collection of traditional English plants in his expansive cottage garden.

Sally's dad, a confirmed atheist who loudly protested and detested organised religion, *'the bloody church'*, had had a surprisingly strong friendship with Stanley. It was ostensibly founded on their mutual passion for all things garden. Compost, manure, seeds, bulbs, and cuttings. They also enjoyed listening to recorded organ music lubricated by a mutual weakness for fortified wines. Her Dad would say, 'Stan's a really good bloke, especially for a poofta and a priest. He's got a good heart, a good ear, and knows how to keep his mouth shut. Never preaches. Knows it's a bloody waste of time with me anyway. Treats everyone the same. The only bullshit you get around him is in his bloody garden.'

Stanley had helped both Brian and their father as each struggled with her brother's homosexuality, impressing on them the importance of living one's own truth; a serious challenge in an historically conservative small country township with a culture of appearances and social standing informing choices. He is also the only person who knows the truth behind Sally's marriage, how and why it happened, what it has become. He has always been there for her. Never preaching or patronising. Ever listening, consoling, and supporting her resolutions, her choices. A true friend. Their meetings have mostly been unplanned; coffee or a pot of tea in the garden, Sally dropping off samples of her baking or preserves. He has phoned her at home but never visited.

"Out of hospital today?" she nods.

"Not ready to go home?" she shakes her head and smiles.

"Have somewhere in mind to stay? Other than here of course. You know you're always welcome." She nods.

"I'll visit Brian and Milton. I have no plans, no idea what I want; only that I can't live with Andy anymore." She sighs. He smiles. "I want my own life. But I don't know what that is."

Stanley looks at his watch and picks up her bag. "Maybe now you're ready to find out. In the car with you. We can be at the rail terminal in twenty minutes and still have time for a latte." He opens the hatchback and stows her bag. "C'mon Emma. In the back."

# Chapter 2

Thursday night

Sally has been waiting for over an hour when Milton bustles into the foyer lounge.

"God Sal, it's you!" he exclaims. "When reception told me a woman was waiting for me, I thought it was this frightful old tart of a flight attendant from Sydney, and decided if I kept her waiting long enough, she'd piss off." He flaps both hands dramatically in front of him. "She has this fanciful notion that I'll escort her to the Casino, and I'm absolutely not up for it; not tonight, not ever! I'd have been here earlier if I'd known it was you."

He stands before her; tall, slim, confident and sophisticated; and leans forward to place a gentle hand on her shoulder.

"Please tell me you've left the beast at last."

Exhaustion has taken over and Sally extends a hand instead of standing for the mandatory warm hug and cheek kisses that usually define their greetings.

"I guess I have." She says. "I haven't been home for two weeks and ... somehow... today... I just couldn't ."

"Where have you been? Why didn't you phone?" He looks at his watch. "Hang on. Where have you parked the car? Um, where are you staying?"

She hesitates, unsure which question to answer, gasps, exhales raggedly and begins to silently weep. She lifts her hand to her face, a finger and thumb squeezing at the tears in each eye before sliding down her nose to pinch closed her nostrils now filling with teary snot.

"Don't move." Milton hands her a perfectly laundered fine white cotton handkerchief, places a compassionate hand on her arm and returns to the hotel reception. Slipping behind the counter with polished familiarity, he speaks quietly over the shoulder of a petite uniformed brunette, watching as she taps rapidly and confidently on the computer keyboard. Returning, he picks up her overnight bag, and with a hand under her elbow, guides her to the lift, holding her gently to him as they ascend silently to the twelfth floor. A slick flick of plastic card has the hotel room door open and Sally inside before she has time to consider where she is or what is happening.

"I don't want to be any trouble. I couldn't get hold of Brian and I knew you'd be working. So much has happened, and now I'm feeling exhausted." Milton guides her gently into the sumptuous black soft leather settee, places a satin cushion behind her back and has a brandy, ice, and soda in her hand in less than two minutes. Deftly popping the cork on a mini-wine bottle he pours himself a bubbly white wine in a long-stemmed flute that he instinctively selects from the shelf above the kitchenette bench. He might well be in his own home, given the ease with which he moves around the space, acquiring exactly what he wants as if by magical design.

"You can start talking, or not, as you please, when you have drunk at least half that brandy. I don't know when you last ate but I'm famished." Lifting the telephone handset, he speaks with warm authority to someone ensconced in the bowels of the twenty-story, central city building. Ten minutes later, while Sally is using the bathroom, a gentle knock on the door heralds the arrival of a trolley bearing an antipasto plate and one of fruit, nuts, and cheese, along with a silver bucket of ice, a bottle of brandy, two bottles of soda water and a bottle of sparkling white wine. Neatly placed to one end are fine china side plates, crisp white linen table napkins and desert forks, accompanied by a silver jug of milk, a glass bowl of dark chocolate truffles and another of assorted coffee pods for the espresso machine resting on the kitchenette counter. Sally gazes in wonder at the sophisticated assortment of snacks and smiles. Trust Milton to do everything with an exquisite attention to detail and style, regardless of the circumstances.

He refills his flute from the new bottle of wine, savouring a sip before replenishing Sally's brandy, and handing her a plate and napkin. His long slender fingers ferry multimorsels to his own plate as he settles back into the damask tub chair.

"I listen best when I am fed" he beams, "and talk best when I'm pissed. Right now is the time for the former." She laughs. The first brandy has settled her. The second is kindling a relaxing warm glow radiating in all directions from her centre. She studies the food selection and chooses a wedge of melting brie, a rolled slice of prosciutto, a couple of dates and three slices from the delicate fan of rock melon.

"Well, well, Sally Anne;" says Milton when she has completed her summary of the past two weeks. "Blood transfusions, a hysterectomy, the bus, the train, a joy ride to freedom with our favourite poofta priest, and taxi rides thrown in each end. I don't suppose you managed to slot in a couple of matinees and some shopping while you were about it." She laughs, unzips her overnight bag, and ceremoniously drapes her purchases across the back of the settee.

"Love the jeans darling. Not so sure about the runners. They are so Kmart."

She laughs again. "Well that's probably because they are."

"You're staying here tonight. And for as long as you need. Until you've decided what you want to do. Brian's away. He's investigating a fly-in, fly-out business proposition in Broome. Did he tell you? No; probably not." He grins and leans back, easing the soft black leather shoes from his feet, exposing a pair of lilac lamb's wool socks beneath the gunmetal grey of his business suit trousers.

"In fact, if you don't mind, I'll stay here with you. I often stay over when he's away or our work shifts are out of sync. It's one of the perks of the job; so you don't have to worry about paying for anything or your name being on the hotel register. That is if you are at all worried about Andy knowing where you are." He pauses to savour a swallow of wine then adds, "That man is such a fucking peasant."

She is surprised; not only because he rarely swears, but also the ferocious change in the tone of his voice.

"Sorry Sal. Few things get me raging, well apart from Johnny Howard. The way that arsehole has neglected you and the boys, just taken you all for granted, appreciating you less than his bloody dogs. It seriously pisses me off." He takes another long, soothing swallow of wine. "It's no wonder Matt and Benjie never want to go home." He pauses; thinking with affection about his lover's nephews. "The upside of course, is that we get to have them with us more often. I so love having them around." They relax into the comfortable relationship they have always had, chatting about the boys, Brian's new business opportunity and purposely avoiding any further references to Andy.

Milton glances at his watch. "God; it's nearly one thirty. You need to rest. And I need my beauty sleep! You have the king in the bedroom; I'll sleep on the settee out here." He waves his hand dismissively. "It's much more comfortable than it looks. Truly! Now I'll just tidy up a bit and you get yourself to bed." He stands and flaps his hands at her. "Shoo! We'll sort what needs to be sorted in the morning". There is no contest from Sally. Within minutes she is in her nighty and stretched out luxuriously between the white steam-pressed sheets. It feels so good, so safe, and somehow, so normal.

* * *

Friday morning

Sally thinks she hears the hospital meal trolley approaching. Opening her eyes, noting the luxuriousness of her surroundings, she remembers where she is, and why. Her watch shows nine-thirty. She has slept through and now desperately needs to pee.

Milton calls gently from the living room. "You awake Sal? Coffee and croissants in three minutes. And I have a couple of my slaves dropping by later." His slaves are his young protégés, to whom he is a professional, cultural, and sometimes personal mentor, helping them to attain casual work to supplement their otherwise meagre allowances while studying. Some are hospitality and tourism students; others are at theatre, film, or music schools. As the Ambassador International Hotel's Function Manager, Milton is always looking for enthusiastic young casual staff he can rely on for large conventions or especially discreet smaller ones. Sally has long understood that he and her brother Brian, a chef who has recently abandoned the stress and toil of restaurant kitchens, live in a radically different world.

"Now which of these little poppets do you fancy?" Milton is holding the bowl of coffee capsules. "They are the special ones for special people on special occasions." He grins affectionately. "That's why I had them sent up last night."

She sits back in her tub chair and gazes in wonder at the breakfast arrangements on what is obviously the replacement trolley. Assorted fruits and a new antipasto platter, an exotic selection of yoghurts and fruit, cereals and a generous jug of milk. A smaller tray disports mini jars of gourmet jam, butter in a petite shallow glass dish and clotted cream in a matching bowl.

The microwave pings and Milton places a cup of steaming milk under the coffee machine spout, deftly pressing the buttons that release the aromatic brew she has chosen. He is wearing a pair of cream slacks with an open-necked royal blue shirt; the long sleeves rolled up midway between wrist and elbow and sees Sally noting his change to casual clothes.

"I have a mini wardrobe in my locker;" he thrusts his hips slightly forwards, theatrically brushing the back of one hand across his brow in a classic drag queen pose. "Well, a wardrobe masquerading as a locker in my office." They both laugh. While unashamedly gay, Milton does not usually present as overtly effeminate. She has never seen him in drag; or ever seen anyone in drag for that matter. She can't imagine him doing so.

"In my job I need a change of clothes for every occasion, and this is my damsel in distress rescue attire. Now, except for coffee, which is never hot enough, use room service whenever you can," he beams. "Then you don't have to wash your own dishes, prepare your own food or worry about smelly leftovers in the bin. I have heated our own croissants though. I do like them hot," and with a theatrical wave of the food tongs, he drops one onto a dessert plate and places it in front of her.

"Butter? Jam? Cream? All three perhaps? Enjoy."

It is a surprisingly carefree and frivolous breakfast and Sally finds herself giggling at his constant chatter about nothing of any consequence, just entertaining incidents, observations, and frustrations of his life in the fast lanes of this giant hotel. When they have eaten and placed their used plates back on the trolley he wheels it into the corridor, presses a few keys on the phone handset and sits purposefully across from her. She knows that they are about to get down to the business of the day.

"Now Sal, without getting too personal about your women's bits or those that have been removed, do you need anything? I mean,... um;... oh God;... I so don't know about this women's stuff. But you only left the hospital yesterday.

Are you alright?" His loving concern for her well-being is etched on his face.

She smiles. "I'm fine. I'm still a little sore, but I've no dressings or medications to worry about." She touches his arm and grins. "And thank you Milton for asking."

"Right. That's out of the way. I haven't spoken to Brian, but I will if you want me to."

"Not yet."

"Are you planning on contacting the Arsehole? He must be at least a little curious as to where you are."

"I don't want to talk to him. I turned my mobile off yesterday after I failed to get hold of Brian. I won't be turning it back on. Stanley showed me how to deactivate my voicemail so he can't leave me messages. I can't bear even the thought of hearing his voice, his drunken abuses. But he needs to know that I'll not be going home."

"Are you absolutely sure about that? I mean, God, Brian and I have so lived in hope; for years." He raises both hands above his head. "I've never understood what has kept you there Sal." She sits still, eyeing the carpet, raises her head and looks directly at him.

"I am not going back. I can't go back. And I want him to *know* that." She sighs, "And I can't have him harassing the boys. They especially must be separated from any fall-out, and there'll sure as hell be some. I think I need another coffee."

Taking her fine china cup he holds out the bowl of pods for her to make another selection before busying himself with his barista duty.

"Is he likely to get ugly? I mean, I know he has had a bit of a reputation for the odd bar fight and was pretty violent on the football ground. Not that I ever saw him mind you. Brian's told me stories." He holds out her coffee and proffers the crystal bowl of last night's chocolates truffles. "You can stay here for now, and you're welcome to stay with us in Grannie's house for as long as you want; but he does know where it is. You'd be on your own when Brian and I are working, and our hours are pretty chaotic." He laughs. "We even have to make appointments to be with each other sometimes."

Grannie's house, so named after Milton's fabulously eccentric grandmother who left it to him, is a comfortable, somewhat bedraggled Federation style house in South Perth just a few streets from Wesley College where her boys have been boarding these past four years. He and Brian pressured her to place them there because of its proximity to their home as well as the yacht club that serves their sailing endeavours along the Swan River. It is her haven away from home, where she always stays when visiting the boys, and where they have relaxed quality time together during school holidays. It is where she most wishes to retreat to, but this time it's not a safe option.

"He's always been difficult, been incredibly selfish. He isn't physically violent with me." She's intent on not lying but uncomfortably close to her truth. "He's become increasingly abusive, especially when he's drunk." She pauses, remembering, choosing her words carefully. "He's been worse these last three years since Margaret died. She indulged him, managed him.. Even after her stroke." She takes a truffle and bites into it, reflecting on her husband's historical behaviours and choices, translating them into his potential response to her leaving. And leaving now. Milton remains silent, his heart open, surrounding her with love.

"I think he could get ugly, although I'm not actually afraid of him. And I don't think he would do anything really stupid. You know, with guns or anything. I mean, he has got some, but he's always been pretty definite about gun safety and being responsible with them".

Milton gives her a quizzical look. "You really sure about that?"

She hesitates. "Well, if I ask myself if I trust him with a gun when he is really angry, or really drunk,... No I'm not." She eats the other half of the truffle, all the while staring pensively into the carpet. She looks up and straight into Milton's eyes. "He is capable of insane, irrational violence, given the right provocation." There. She's said it.

They sip on their coffees, thinking, looking at each other, one searching for a solution, the other intent on blocking memories. Milton leans forward and begins toying with the box of silver coasters sitting on the coffee table.

"I can feel a plan coming on. Tell me if my take on this is off the mark. You want him to know you won't be going home. You don't wish to speak to him. You don't want him to know where you are. You can't go to Grannies house. We can't be sure it's safe. You don't want the boys to be caught up in any of it."

He has placed a coaster down firmly on the table as he stated each point. He stands and gazes out the window as if directions are about to pop up on a billboard. Sally leans back into the chair and takes another sip of coffee. She has nothing to say.

"The boys will need to know of course but you can probably keep it from them for a few days yet. Do they ever talk to their dad? Do they ring him? Does he contact the school?"

"No to all three," she sighs. "He asks me what they are doing, when they are coming home, when they visit you and Brian and what you might all have got up to. He never phones them, never asks them what they've been doing or shows any interest in them, other than what they should be doing around the farm when they come home." Another long suffering sigh. "If either of them had played football or cricket it might have been different. But they've only ever been interested in hockey and tennis; none of their father's competitive sports." She pauses. "And I'm sure that was a joint calculated decision. Their father has been the role model of all they don't want to be."

Right," says Milton, sitting once again. He leans forward, his hands clasped and forearms resting on his knees. "First up is to protect them; keep them out of firing range. How old are they? Um, Sixteen? Or is it seventeen in December?"

"Seventeen," replies Sally. "They are going to be most concerned about me, actually. They've never been close to their father. They learned early that they could never depend on him. His moods frightened them when they were very little. They now pursue total avoidance and have become increasingly adept at it." She smiles a sad and weary smile. "While they say nothing, I see their concern for me in their eyes. I know they despise him." Her voice quavers as an unexpected moment of grief overtakes her.

Milton stands, takes a couple of measured steps back towards the window, turns and waggles his long slender forefinger at nothing in particular.

"Control, not custody, is the immediate priority. Brian and I sail with the Bursar at Wesley. I'll give him a call, explain the situation, find out what can be done about screening the boys from any phone calls or untimely visits should he try to get at you through them. I'm sure this won't be the first time they've been faced with this situation." He stands beside her and places a gentle caring hand on her shoulder. "You need to get a message to him. Any attempt at a phone call will be pointless; from you, or me, or Brian. A letter will take too long. What do you want to say to him anyway?"

"I'm not coming home. It's finished."

"It?.... Not we?" he enquires with genuine surprise. "That's all?" He raises both hands in disbelief. "Well I'm sure I could find a few more things to say to the contemptable peasant." He notes the flicker of concern on her face. "Don't worry. I'll behave." She walks into the bedroom, returning, her wallet in hand, and takes out a postcard she bought the day before. Milton watches as she writes a brief message in bold capital letters.

"Will that do?" she smiles. He takes the postcard and holds it at arm's length, turning it both ways. On one side is Bart Simpson, in red shirt with blue shorts around his ankles, bending over to show a bare bum. And on the other Sally's message.

*"Andy. I am not coming home.*
*IT IS FINISHED.*
*Sal."*

He is temporarily speechless, looking at her in astonishment. She laughs.

"The boys so love the Simpsons. I bought that as a joke to send to them. In an envelope of course!"

"Well, I approve of both messages' He too laughs. "But it doesn't really give any indication that it's actually from you. I mean, this doesn't look like you or your handwriting.

It could be me for instance, pretending to be you. How will he know, it is, actually, from you?"

She opens her wallet and draws out a small business size laminated card and hands it across the coffee table. On it is a pale photo of a man in white trousers and gold singlet, legs astride, swinging an axe at an upright log. Superimposed over the top in bold black print is 'Preston Districts Axemen's Club', and on the other side, 'Sally Chester; Associate member.'

"You? A member of the axemen's club?"

She laughs. "Take a closer look at the photo they've used on the card?" Milton squints, his forehead creasing in a frown of concentration; then holds it out in front of him, his head askance.

"Well pluck a duck. It's the Arsehole." He snorts derisively. "He had a bit more hair then."

"The main reason I'm registered as an associate member is because his photo was used on the card. He was club champion for five years straight. I always knew it was a sort of a 'Take this, bitch,' statement. And with the card comes the privilege of discounted drinks at all their functions. I mostly manage to keep that to one a year when he uses me to save face in front of the other wives. It's easier to go sit with them, talk about kids and cooking or nothing in particular than to put up with his haranguing or sulks. That's the only reason it has stayed in my wallet."

"Well we need to put these two together and get them to him somehow," says Milton. "Posting them will take too long. Delivering them to him at home is a bit iffy; and potentially dangerous for whoever gets to complete the deed. From what you say he's become like a firecracker just waiting to go off and this promises to be just the spark to do it."

She leans over and retrieves the card, placing it neatly on top of the postcard in the centre of the coffee table.

"The Railway Hotel is the best bet. He's there at some time most days and *always* on Friday night." She looks knowingly at Milton. They both laugh.

"Well," he coos, "That makes tonight the night, then!" There is a jolly and rhythmic knock on the door. He strides over, opening it with a grand sweep of his hand.

"And right on cue, I present, Gregory Patterson." He peers outside. "Is Shane with you?"

"Sure is," pipes a theatrically high-pitched voice from the corridor; and two young men, both in their early twenties, saunter in. The second is wheeling the breakfast trolley before him.

"We're starving. Didn't have time for breakfast after you called. Went for a two-hour sail off Fremantle this morning. Bloody fantastic. I take it these are leftovers!" Neither waits for a reply as they help themselves to fruit and cereal.

"Ahem. Excuse me, gentlemen," orders Milton; and both tall lean men slowly stand to attention. "I'd like you to meet my sister-in-law, Sally Anne Chester." Sally stands to shake both their hands and grins.

"Just call me Sal. Everyone does and I prefer it. Sally Anne was only ever used when I'd displeased my dad."

"Sorry," groans Greg as he extends a hand, "I'm Greg by the way. We truly didn't mean to be rude. Too caught up in the energy of the morning; and we had no idea we were being summoned for a *family* mission." He glares at Milton.

"Please eat," laughs Sally. "I'm the last person to keep two starving men from a meal." Greg and Shane are both over six feet, tanned, lean and with dusky blonde hair, obviously bleached by the sea and the sun. They are also obviously twins and Sally guesses they're sailing club colleagues as well as Milton's slaves. She watches with amusement as they help themselves to all the treats on the trolley. Milton raises his eyebrows and rolls his eyes in a theatrical gesture of social dismay.

"How would you two like to take Valerie on a little adventure in the countryside?" he asks. "Full tank of fuel and fifty dollars travel money each? I'm assuming that neither of you have a car that can currently be relied on to travel more than a suburb or two."

"Done," they both grin, replying in unison.

"Just tell us when and where. Hey, are these left-over coffee capsules too?" asks Gregory as he places a coffee cup under the espresso machine spout. Milton turns to Sally.

"You okay with this Sal, if Greg and Shane deliver your card to the beast this evening? Maybe get there around say,.... five thirty; have a drink, play some of that... What's that billiard thingy game? You do play, don't you?"

"Pool." They chorus together.

"And yes, we do," adds Greg. "Every uni student plays pool! Why else would we go to a pub? Unless there's a decent live band of course?"

"So is that it?" Queries Shane; "The two of us hired to deliver a postcard and this; what is it; business card? Who is this dude anyway?" He peers at the membership card. "I thought we were invited to go on an adventure Millie. Pretty bloody tame if you ask me."

"Actually," says Sally; "I would rather like to get my car and a few things. Now that I think about it. If I'm not going back at all. There's no way I can risk facing Andy... Not now."

She pauses before speaking with a considered seriousness. "That could be a bit tricky. It *will* take some skulduggery."

"Yes!" exclaims Greg, pumping a fist into the air in mock excitement. "I've always wanted to be a Mission Impossible agent. Just once. Now you're talking." Shane, getting into their adrenalin-fuelled party game, begins da da-ing the theme to the television series while rolling his shoulders rhythmically and flat palm drumming the back of a tub chair.

"Heel boys. Let's not get carried away. Sobriety is required here if you don't mind." Milton turns to Sally and asks, "What besides your car can you just not live without for the moment, Sal? We can surely negotiate the collection of your personal belongings down the track." He notes the life-weary, dreary expression on her face. "Well, maybe not. But let's just deal with the now, for now, if you all don't mind;" and he looks intently at each of his visitors.

Glancing at his watch, he turns gently to Sally. "I need to put in a few hours in the office. Why don't you make a list of the essentials; explain to the *boys* here how to get to the farm, how to get in and where everything is. I've organised a split shift for today." He moves purposefully towards the door.

# Chapter 3

Early Friday afternoon

The *boys* are waiting restlessly with Shane's girlfriend, a short, well-rounded, olive-skinned young woman of similar age, dressed in jeans and an oversized flamboyantly coloured and patterned shirt. She has wild curly black hair, dangly silver earrings, and no makeup. The underground car park is well known to them. They stand adjacent to the door where Milton will appear from the bowels of the building to direct them to his car, a slate grey Volvo sports convertible, affectionately known as Valerie. With a black collapsible hood, no wings, or extras, she is quietly sophisticated and immaculate, all Milton.

"Well hello Petal; you along for the ride? I thought you'd be rehearsing today," he says in greeting.

"I would, normally, but they've dropped me out of today's schedule. Anyway, Shane said I'd be needed as an accomplice on this mission. I've met Sal and she's happy for me to pack up her personal things." Greg, the most affable and commanding of the twins, describes their plan to Milton.

"We reckon we'll get there before dark and drive past the farm, so that way we'll know exactly where it is and how long it takes to drive to the Railway Hotel. We'll go for a drink and a few games of pool. Once Mr Chester turns up, Shane and Kelsie will leave and drive back to the farm, grab Sal's stuff, and pick up her car. I'll keep the dude busy; keep him talking or something; give them time to collect everything and get out of there. Shane will come to pick me up from the pub. We'll hand over the message and ske-daddle. Kelsie will wait for us in Sal's car at the first truck stop north of the river to make sure everything has gone as planned before we head home."

"How will you know Andy? How will you recognise him?" asks Milton.

"Sal described him and his farm ute; gave us the rego and explained where he always parks. We'll keep a watch through the bar window. She says it should be in clear view from there." Greg is sounding calm and confident; gone is the bravado and theatrics of the morning. Shane is only half listening, sliding one hand over the sleek mudguards on Valerie and the other over Kelsie's bum.

"You got all this Shane" asks Milton. "We need your mind on the mission matey." Kelsie slaps Shane's hand away and reassures her mentor.

"Don't worry. He'll do as he's told, won't you Shane;" and she pushes him less than gently in the stomach. Milton hands over the envelope addressed to Mr Andrew Chester; pulls out his wallet and removes three fifty-dollar notes.

"I really am just going for the ride Milton. I don't expect to be paid." Kelsie's strength of independence asserts itself.

"Drinks and supper;" he smiles. "You're worth every cent. These two clowns need someone with common sense to remind them what they're meant to be doing. I'm actually relieved you're tagging along. And I know you won't let either of them push Valerie here over the speed limit. That right boys?" He gives his Volvo a gentle pat as he hands over the keys. "And no food or drinks in Valerie thank you. I don't want her smelling like a week-old wheelie bin."

The afternoon drags on for Sally. Milton has returned to work, and she can't find anything on any of the in-house television channels to engage her interest. It seems strange to be in the same city as her boys and not in contact with them. She phones them every Sunday. They're always happy to talk with her, reassure her as to their individual and joint well-being; and tell minor tales on each other. Any questions are mostly those for which they already have the answers; rarely anything about their father. They seem to be typical seventeen-year-olds, intent on their own lives and their place in the clearly defined world they live in, with only a polite interest in the place they have come from.

She is always cheerful and encouraging, never hinting at the dreariness of her days or the constant irritability and moroseness that now defines their father's disposition. The news she shares with them reflects her mundane daily reality. It includes: the level of the creek after rain, antics the farm dogs have got up to, the first buddings of field mushrooms; the first dropping of calves in autumn and lambs in spring. There is the occasional mention of an elderly neighbour the boys know who is sick or has passed away, a property sold, the old bakery turned into a café come gift shop, lightening hitting the Catholic Church; and Barney who lives in the old army hut at the base of the railway bridge, setting fire to his hut and himself and jumping in the river. She never speaks of their old primary school friends; all social connections having been dislocated once they went to boarding school.

Milton returns for two hours in the late afternoon, dressed once again in his business suit; this time with a smoky grey business shirt, burgundy tie, and matching lamb's wool socks. He smells faintly of a subtle earthy cologne, like aniseed or nutmeg, just as the peppermint smell of toothpaste lingers after someone has just cleaned their teeth. He is relaxed and attentive, enveloping Sally in his affectionate concern for her comfort. She agrees, with his quiet encouragement, to stay in the hotel for the time being until they have a better idea of what she wants to do. Her car will be garaged downstairs for her. She is both impressed and grateful for the obvious power and privileges his senior position affords him.

He is no longer moving, talking, or thinking at the energetic pace that had defined his imposing organisational manner earlier in the day. She welcomes the change. Confident that despite their youth, the slaves and Kelsie will complete their mission appropriately, Milton is enormously relieved that Sally has made this move at last and tells her so. He and Brian have long been aware of her suffocating situation. Neither had realised that she had been so unwell. While she'd appeared tired and distracted at times, they'd put this down to the depression and misery of life with the Arsehole.

"I spoke to Brian earlier," he says. "I know you wanted to wait till he returns from Broome, but we talk every day, and I couldn't not tell him. He's your only sibling. He needs to know. And we have no secrets between us. Never have. He'll be on the first flight tomorrow morning."

"What did he say?"

"Quote, 'Well thank bloody Christ for that!' He is seriously concerned for your physical well-being as well as how you're feeling emotionally. We've been really worried about you Sal, for a very long time."

"I'm fine; on both grounds. I am always so damned organised, planning everything to the last detail. This has surprised even me." She pauses, thinking over the incongruity of yesterday's choices and behaviours. "It was as if a second me I have forgotten about, a protective twin sister, just took over and brought me here."

Milton laughs: "So who am I sitting with and talking to now?"

"I'm not sure. I'm not even sure what I'm feeling. Relief? Disbelief? I think the separation and solitude I had in hospital has been a transition from the before to now. Do you know what I mean? And I feel so much stronger. I had no idea that anaemia could be so debilitating. Not just physically, but mentally, emotionally. Like moving through time in a different gear, where everything seems normal, appears normal, but you know that in truth it isn't. And you don't know why."

Milton looks at his watch; "It's 5.30. You want a brandy, a glass of wine? I don't drink when I'm working but I'm going to pour myself a flute of mineral water. Looks and feels like my bubbly without the flavour or the afterglow;" he stands and moves to the kitchenette. "It's too easy to get sucked into an alcoholic abyss in this work. I'm in charge, need to be seen to be in charge, and need to be in control of myself."

"Um." She hesitates. She is not a practised drinker. Since Andy's alcoholism has escalated, his behaviours becoming more erratic and abusive, she has clung fiercely to the control that sobriety affords her. She has not let anything relax or distract her from deflecting his moods, his abuse, his irrationality. But that life is over. "A brandy and soda would be nice;" she smiles.

* * *

Friday evening

The *slaves* pull into the Railway Hotel, in high spirits. They have driven most of the way with the convertible top down and have the wild hair, flushed cheeks and hyperactivity that follows being in a wind tunnel of fresh country air on a warm spring afternoon. Kelsie and Shane jump out and begin smoothing down their hair. Greg stands by waiting for the convertible's hood to manoeuvre itself back into place.

"You know, this is bloody handy. You can leave the top down while you're loading it with some of Sal's gear," he says. Valerie gives a high-pitched hiccup and flashes her indicator lights in agreement as he presses the lock button on the ignition keys.

"A Scotch or a beer, a Scotch or a beer. That is the question," he croons.

They sit on stools at the bench under the window that looks out to the highway from the public bar. They are perfectly positioned to see the parking space for Andy's ute across the road under the towering gum trees that originally sat in the yard of the station masters house. That has long gone, as well as the station buildings. The railway platform remains, and they can see the giant oak tree in its centre, planted from an acorn nearly a century ago, on the day a steam train left with a handful of fresh-faced farm boys volunteering for the First World War.

Andy's farm ute is already in place. Shit. They will have to watch the men at the bar and listen in to conversations. By the time they have bought their second drinks there is still no sign of him. All three are beginning to fidget. Kelsie and Shane don't want to leave until they are certain he isn't back at the farm. Maybe his ute has broken down and he's got a lift home. Not likely. Is there another drinking space in the hotel? Kelsie checks when she goes looking for a toilet. There *is* another upmarket bar at the end of the large lounge dining room, but the dress and behavioural expectations are obviously higher than those tolerated in the worker's bar. All the drinkers are sitting at dining tables or in the clusters of tub lounge chairs placed around low tables. She can't imagine Andy drinking there.

"Let's order a counter meal," she says when she returns, "I'm starving." The wall menu displays the usual pub fare. Schnitzels, steaks, battered fish; all with chips and salad, steak burger, roast of the day, and something called a "Super Dog." On enquiry that turns out to be a hot dog with absolutely everything.

"I'll have one of those," says Shane; "Just to add to the adventure. It's been pretty bloody tame so far. In fact I'm starting to get bored. Bugger all this waiting and inaction." Greg leans on the bar to place their orders. He is going for a beef schnitzel and Kelsie the fish. And yes, she can have pan-fried unbattered fish with chips and salad. They now order soft drinks. No more alcohol until this mission is finished and they're back in the city.

"Hey, I don't suppose Andy Chester is here," Greg asks the bar attendant; a sullen, oversized, blonde farm girl poured into bulging undersized jeans. She is unkindly referred to by the public bar clientele as 'Bella the Barmaid'. She is obviously not embracing her Friday night's agenda, having been called in at short notice when the proprietor's wife needed to attend to *other duties*.

"He's the uncle of a mate of mine," says Greg casually, "and I thought I'd buy him a drink if he's here." She stares at him blankly and exchanges a quizzical look with the old man leaning over his beer on the bar next to him. They both know Andy Chester has no siblings and no nephews. The old man takes a measured look at Greg, grunts, and turns to stare at his companions.

"He's here. He's out the back," Bella pauses, "on business."

"Yeah. Monkey business," drawls the old man. "Probably chockers right now." He drains his glass and taps it meaningfully on the bar. Bella glares at him and turns to look behind her at the clock.

"He'll be in shortly, she says, "He usually has a counter meal about seven."

"Bugger," says Chelsie, drinking the last mouthful of her coke. "We'll have to finish our counter meals before we can leave. We've lost daylight. And we can't just sit here drinking Colas." She looks out the window. "And we're seriously losing time. I mean how long can we expect him to stay drinking after his meal. My Dad never drinks after he's eaten. So the silly old bugger defers eating, gets pissed and then Mum gets pissed off at him." She gives a throaty laugh.

Shane polishes off his 'Super Dog' in record time and helps Kelsie finish her chips. He sculls his Coke and belches loudly.

"Don't you dare fart;" she glares. "Not now or in the car. Well, not unless you put the roof down." They leave Greg chatting to a couple of young men playing pool who have just invited him to join them. Shane slaps her on the bum and calls out to his brother.

"We'll catch you later." She notices the pool players laughing and looking suggestively at each other. As they stand in front of Valerie, Shane fumbling to pull the keys from his back pocket, she turns and pushes him fiercely.

"Just because we've been in the bloke's bar doesn't give you licence to behave like Macho Man. Don't you dare make out I'm your bitch." She is furious and stamps her feet, waiting irritably for him to unlock Valerie. If this had been Shane's old Falcon instead of Milton's Volvo, she'd likely have kicked a dent in its door. Simultaneously, they bend and lower themselves into the soft leather car seats.

"Sorry Kel. I didn't mean it. I just got caught up in the mood of the place. You know, immersing myself in the local culture. Just a country version of theatre sports." He leans across to plant a kiss on her cheek. She intercepts him with the palm of her hand and pushes his face away.

"Well just warn me next time." She squeezes out a cheeky grin and Shane knows he's been forgiven. He starts up the engine, looking at her intently, the engine purring quietly as the convertible hood folds down. He continues to gaze at her with measured adoration as he lets out a long, loud, piercing fart before backing out onto the highway and heading north. Kelsie slaps his thigh, glaring at him with a cocktail of revulsion, disbelief, amusement, and affection. By the time they turn right after the bridge half a kilometre away they are both giggling uncontrollably.

\* \* \*

Greg knows exactly when Andy enters the bar. There are a variety of greetings reflecting the crowd that is exclusively male, apart from Bella whose gender is obviously ignored in their boorish blokey behaviours.

"Ya worked up a thirst Andy old son? Ya must be hanging out for a fucking beer."

"Take a seat, Andy. You're lookin' weak in the knees mate."

"Ah leave the man alone you bastards. A beer for me and me mate here; Bella." The old man pulls out a stool for Andy and drains the glass he's been cradling. Greg and his fellow players return to their game.

"You want the usual?" queries Bella as she places Andy's beer on the bar in front of him and nods back to the bar menu displayed behind her.

"He's already had that," bellows a long skinny freckled fellow as he tugs his darts out of the board attached to the far wall.

"Aw. Fuck off you bastards. I'm not in the mood;" growls Andy, and he drains his glass in just three swallows, sitting the empty down assertively on the bar. Message received. As one, the crowd resumes their previous postures, conversations, drinking, pool and dart games.

"Nah," says Andy, "I'll have the Super Dog tonight. And give us another beer."

Greg opts out of the next pool game and sits with his Cola back near the window, watching Andy chew through his hot dog. He can't decide if he is ravenously hungry or just a slob, as he watches him take a giant bite, filling his mouth to capacity and chewing clumsily. He wipes the slime of grease and sauce from his chin with the back of his hand, transferring it to the bar towel. The only time he pauses is when he needs to pick sticky strings of shredded lettuce or morsels of beetroot or bacon from his checked farm shirt. Jesus, what a pig. Greg looks up at the bar clock. Shane and Kelsie should be well into their mission by now.

"Hey Andy," a big bald bloke calls from the side door as he rolls his beer belly into the bar. "I see ya missus is home. Saw this flash sports car leavin' a dust trail up your driveway. You makin' more than ya say outta ya tomatas this year?" He looks around at his mates and laughs. "Or is she just catchin' a ride home with that flash jack brother a hers?" Andy looks up blankly and places his glass down gently on the bar. As far as people know, because he's told them, Sally is still in hospital. He and the old man and his son said nothing when they'd seen her driven off in the bus yesterday. It was as if it had been a mutual imagining as they silently finished their drinks and went home.

"Hey Bella. Pass me the phone." The farm phone rings out. Andy switched off the answering machine yesterday, not wanting Sal to see the red light blinking his neglect. He drains his glass, holding it as he rests it firmly on the bar, frowning and obviously deliberating on this latest news

Shit. Greg looks at the clock again. Andy is just sitting there in contemplative silence. What about the letter. He watches as Andy stands, gives his trousers a hitch and pushes the bar stool aside. Greg pulls the letter from his back pocket and walks purposefully across to the bar.

"Excuse me Mr Chester," he says in what he hopes is a casual and agreeable manner. "I've been asked to give you this." He stands back politely as Andy takes it, looks at his formal name on the envelope, looks contemptuously back at Greg and pulls it open. The flap has been tucked in; the envelope not sealed. The membership card falls to the floor as he removes the post card. He bends to pick it up, recognising it immediately. He turns the postcard over and reads Sally's message.

"Fuckin' bitch." Placing both cards on the bar he glares at Greg. "And who would you be?"

"Just a messenger." Greg is determined to remain casual and friendly but wonders if he is about to be whacked or shoved up against the wall. "I was asked to pass this on to you if I saw you, and I've seen you. That's all. I have to go now Mr Chester. Good night," He walks in measured casual steps across to the side door, steps outside, waiting anxiously for it to close, then runs frantically to the safety of the outdoor toilets, skidding on a wet patch on the concrete and saving himself as he grabs the door frame. He snatches a quick glance back to the bar to see if he's been followed. He hasn't.

"He had two friends with him before," says Bella to Andy. "They left a while ago; just before you walked in. I thought something was fishy when he asked about you earlier; said you were the uncle of a mate of his." Andy strides fiercely out the door. The silence in the bar is broken by the sound of his ute spinning loose stones as he backs out of his parking space, the engine screaming in protest as he accelerates through the gears. Bella picks up the postcard and reads it. A wide grin expands slowly across her face as she looks out across the dickheads she has been serving for the last three hours.

"Now here's one for the pool room," she says, planting a silent kiss on the postcard before polishing it gently on the bulbous bosom bouncing beneath her T-shirt. She places it triumphantly on the mirror backed trophy shelf above the cash register, resting it gently against the biggest one in central place. This is the Axeman of the Year trophy that has sat there in majestic prominence for over a decade. Everyone knows that Andy's name is engraved on it more times than anyone else's; in fact more than the rest of them put together.

At that moment, the proprietor's wife struts purposefully into the room, and with an air of measured authority, places herself behind the bar. She has obviously come straight from her boudoir. Her short copper and blonde streaked hair is held perfectly in spiky place with product. Her make-up is immaculate, her tailored turquoise shirt, collar fashionably raised at the back, is pulled firmly over pert breasts and tucked neatly into tailored white linen slacks. A platted gold belt defines her skinny little waist.

Bella kisses Sally's membership card gently as she looks mockingly into her boss's eyes, polishes it slowly on her bosom and leans it gently against the postcard.

"On ya Sal!" she murmurs quietly. She presses a key on the cash register to release the cash drawer and pulls out a crisp new hundred-dollar note. "My wages," she says sarcastically, again staring straight at her boss. Slapping it dramatically on the bar she yells, *"Okay you miserable bastards, the drinks are on me!"* and rolls her great bosom and bulging buttocks out the side door.

\* \* \*

Greg is sitting on the toilet seat punching at the keys on his phone. "Oh fuck. Oh fuck. Oh fuck. Pick up Shane." He has already left a message. "Get outta there *now*! The arsehole is on his way, and he is *not happy*!" If only he had wheels. How far is it to the farm? He is fit, and a runner. How long will it take to sprint there? Too long. It's a comfortable five-minute drive if you slow down for the dip at the single-lane bridge over the creek; and what if Shane and Kelsie drive straight past him? They won't know where to find him. He decides to wait under the gum trees near Andy's parking place and slinks his way across the highway, taking extra care not to be seen.

# Chapter 4

Friday night

Kelsie gives Shane the lead as he finds a pathway through the debris of boots, buckets, and boxes that litter the area around the back door of the farmhouse. A long raincoat, sundry hats and beanies and a West Coast Eagles footy jumper hang from hooks on the adjacent wall. Turning the door handle, he finds it unlocked, as expected, and runs his hand up and down, locating both the kitchen and verandah light switches. He turns them both on. Two anxious and excited kelpie dogs are chained to the end verandah posts. Shane rips the lids off two cans of dog food discovered amongst the tatters of cardboard cartons that lie in disarray around them. He talks to them jovially as he fills each of their bowls while allowing them to sniff his hands, his shoes, and his legs. He guesses they haven't been fed for a while and tops up each of their water buckets from the hose snaking lazily across the adjacent patch of lawn.

He and Kelsie give themselves a quick orientation of the layout of the house, confirming the descriptions Sally has given them. The phone rings. They stand staring at each other in silence as it rings out.

"I'm not comfortable with all these lights on," she says. "What if someone drives past and sees them? I'm getting Sal's keys and backing her car out of the carport. I want it next to the side gate so I can just drive out if we have to leave in a hurry. You should do the same with Valerie."

Sally's car keys are exactly where she'd said. Kelsie can see that she is a very ordered and organised person, and despite the chaotic filth left by Andy, the house is clearly well cared for. It is an old weatherboard farmhouse with verandahs on three sides; the fourth having been enclosed for a bathroom, laundry and sleep-out. Timber dados painted the same colour as the rest of the walls seemed to have been left in each room except the kitchen, which was probably renovated less than a decade ago. It has a double sink, dishwasher, six burner gas stove as well as the old Agar wood stove built into the brick fireplace. Sally is obviously an accomplished cook. The appliances and their placement are not just for show. They look well used.

When she returns, she finds Shane opening the fridge and hastily closing it before poking through the mail piled up on the kitchen bench. He is so easily distracted.

"You get the computer off Sal's desk and the sewing machine from the sleep-out," she commands. "It's through the French doors off the dining room. Her photo albums are in the lounge room bookcase. I'll pack her mother's dinner set into a carton, or maybe a case; easier to carry. Can you see any newspaper anywhere?' And she begins opening cupboards.

"Just use some towels or something;" Shane calls from the lounge room. "Easy to find and probably better. Sal said she has cases on top of her wardrobe. That's in the second bedroom. Seems she and the Arsehole haven't shared a bed for a while."

"Not our business Shane. Now get to it. I've left the backup on Sal's car. You might as well put them in her boot rather than Valerie. I'm glad she has an automatic. I've not driven a geared car since I got my licence."

"Christ; what's that bloody stink?" he groans.

"There's rotten tomatoes and potatoes in the crates near the carport, and I think those bags stacked near the fence and in the trailer are filled with poo. He grows vegies or something doesn't he?"

Kelsie enters Sally's bedroom and is surprised to see that she sleeps in an old wrought iron double bed with a crocheted cotton cover. It is quite a girly room. The furniture is seriously old and includes a colonial spindle rocking chair near the window. All of it including the walls, are painted white; the soft furnishings providing the colour. There is a stainless steel barrel bolt lock on the inside door, and another on the French doors to the verandah. She pulls two cases down from the top of the wardrobe and taking the smaller one into the lounge room, lays it open in front of the glass cabinet. Pillowcases and hand towels are easily located in the linen cupboard in the hallway and she begins to methodically pack the small collection of old china and crystal.

Shane returns and asks, "You see my phone? I thought I heard it ringing but I can't find it."

"You took it out of your back pocket and put it with your wallet in Valerie's console. Here, take this and I'll just pack a few of Sal's clothes." She hands him the case and turns to peer out the window. "Are they lights coming down the driveway?"

"Oh Shit! Oh hell! Get in your car."

Shane runs behind Kelsie out the backdoor, leaping off the verandah and hastily placing the case into the back seat of Sally's car as Kelsie scrambles into the driver's seat.

"Go! Go! Go! Wait for me at the truck stop!" He slams the boot shut.

His rage compounding as he has driven the few kilometres from the pub, Andy races his ute around behind the back of the carport, parking it so that the headlights shine into the machinery shed. Shane is fumbling in his jeans pockets for Valerie's keys. Shit. They aren't there. Has he left them inside the house or in the ignition? He looks back towards Andy and sees him pushing a red cartridge into each of the two barrels of a shotgun.

"Oh fuck, oh fuck, oh fuck." The same panic mantra as his brother. He is backing away when Andy places the gun to his shoulder and pulls the trigger, the barrel lifting up violently. Shane's feet and lower legs are sprayed with gravel dislodged by shotgun pellets blasting the ground two meters in front of him. He freezes.

"And who the bloody hell might you be, Mr Fancy fuckin' pants in your fancy fuckin' sports car? And where's my wife?" Andy moves towards Shane. The shotgun is now pointing directly at him.

"I think you'll find her inside Mr Chester. We were just bringing her home," he lies, faking both confidence and nonchalance.

"So, who was driving her fuckin' car down the driveway then? She done you a deal or somethin'?" Andy gestures towards Valerie with his shotgun. "Not fuckin' likely. This ain't her kinda car. And I bet she's not inside either, ya lyin' fuckin' little shit." He waves the gun towards the house then points it back at Shane from just three metres away. Shane backs around Valerie. Andy follows him. Should he turn and run towards the machinery shed? Find somewhere to hide? Leg it down the drive or across the paddocks? Nope. Andy has all the advantages.

"I'd feel a lot more comfortable if you'd put your gun down Mr Chester. I know you're angry and I'm sure you have every right to be, your wife running off and all that."

"What do you know about ma fuckin' wife? And where is the fuckin' bitch?" He continues to pace towards Shane, pointing the gun and jerking it upwards each time he poses a question, as though the gun-waving will elicit an answer. "You'll be one of her brother's fuckin' bum boys. This your car then? Or his?" He kicks the rear bumper. "Probably that fuckin' fancy pants boyfriend he shacks up with." He kicks the bumper a second time. "Yep. This is absolutely that fuckin Minty walker's style."

Shane continues backing around the car, Andy following, and has completed a full circuit when he spies the ignition keys sitting snugly in the crevice of the driver's seat. He leans down sideways as if to straighten the leg of his jeans and discretely palms them, rearranging them so that the key is held firmly between his thumb and forefinger, ready to push into the ignition at the first opportunity. Backing slowly around the car, he watches trepidatiously as Andy pursues him in steady calculated steps; the two of them locked in this curious choreography. All the while he tries to covertly detect if there are any potential weapons or missiles within reach. If only he could pick up a crate or a stick in his left hand and swing it at Andy to knock that gun out of his hands.

Andy is staring aggressively at him over the barrel of his gun, exhaling in guttural pants. Shane knows with cortisol clarity how people can piss themselves with fear. This man is a consummate bully; a lunatic. He's obviously been drinking but is not drunk; just totally insane with rage. There is no point in trying to talk him down. There is no escape. How many more revolutions of Valerie does he have before the Arsehole takes him out? He'll have to be bold and do something unexpected.

Pocketing Valerie's keys, he raises his arms in surrender, takes a couple of slow submissive steps towards Andy and then screams, "Fuck the West Coast Eagles!" throwing himself violently forward, head butting Andy in the stomach. The shotgun goes off ear-shatteringly close and he sits in the gravel shaking his head in disbelief, realising, despite the ringing in his ears, that he is still alive. Sheep dags from the bags in the trailer rain down upon them. Andy too is in the dirt, on his back and groaning, the shotgun well away to his side. He has been seriously winded.

It takes a minute or two for Shane to regain his wits. Andy is still groaning. Shane stands, picks up the shotgun, and with both hands grasping the barrel, spins around twice as he attempts to toss it hammer-throwing style into the paddock. His thwarted intention sees it hitting the tank stand and breaking into several pieces. He turns back to look at Andy, almost feeling sorry for him. Taking Valerie's keys from his pocket, he leans forward, extends a hand, and asks, "You alright Mr Chester?"

"Fuck off ya little shit." Andy levers himself up off the ground, wiping the dust off his bum and running both hands across the top of his head.

"Yes, well, I had better be on my way. I do have people waiting for me." Shane wipes the back of his jeans with the palm of his free hand.

"Well, how about you take something for the road," snarls Andy. He picks up a bag of chicken manure and empties it into the back seat. Grabbing a crate of rotting tomatoes, he scatters its contents across the car interior and tosses it aside to bounce carelessly off the fence.

"Aw fuck", groans Shane. "Come on, Mr Chester, that's really not a good idea." Andy reaches for a crate of rotting potatoes and raises it in both hands above his head. Shane cowers; one arm raised to protect the side of his head as he prepares to lower himself into Valerie's driver's seat. The crate comes hurtling towards him. He raises both arms, deflecting the crate so that it bounces off the windscreen and across to Valerie's other side. Potatoes spill into the front seat and rumble across the bonnet. The putrescent stench is immediate. He wipes rotten potato slime from his face with the back of his hand and can see smashed potato splattered across the front seats and windscreen.

As Andy turns, appearing to walk away, Shane jumps into the driver's seat. Several potatoes push up into his bum. He pushes the key into the ignition and turns it, Valerie's engine responding immediately. Lifting his buttocks to dislodge the potatoes, he looks hastily behind him. Andy has a broken bag of manure in each hand. They are raised to his shoulders, swinging unsteadily behind him, spilling sheep pellets from one and clumps of chicken manure from the other where the second gunshot has left tattered holes. Shane pushes the gear stick into drive. Andy swings the bags after him, and as he accelerates, Shane hears them explode onto Valerie's back seats. Andy roars behind him.

"And tell ya fuckin dung punchin' mates there's plenty more shit where this comes from! Ya fuckin' mob a pooftas."

Accelerating down the driveway, Valerie's tail swinging almost out of control, he pulls out onto the road. Jesus. He just needs to get the hell out of there. What a monumental fuckup. The whole exercise. And the car, Milton's baby, his Valerie, brutalised. Where can he pull up to get rid of all that stinking cargo? He is still accelerating as the single-lane bridge at the dip in the road looms ahead of him. Oh Fuck. Easing up too late, he bellies her, the rear bumper hitting the bitumen with a deafening, tearing, grating thud. He can hear it dragging as he slows to a stop. Dropping his head between his hands, he leans forward, collapsing onto the steering wheel.

"Oh fuck, oh fuck, oh fuck," he sobs, a mixture of relief, despair, and absolute disbelief. Never has he felt so desolate and defeated.

* * *

Kelsie knows it is Valerie and Shane as she watches the headlights pull up behind her in the rear vision mirror. He doesn't get out. She turns to look behind. There are no other cars coming. What is keeping him? Leaving Sally's car she walks back to meet him. My god, what a stink. Circling Valerie, she grapples with the sight before her, the moonlight highlighting the cocktail of slime. Tomatoes, crushed and whole; rotten potatoes, sheep pellets, and clumps of grey and white chicken manure with the occasional feather fluttering in the night air, are festooned along the length and breadth of Milton's car. On the seats, on the floor, between the folds of the convertible's roof, and glued to the mudguards and bonnet in glistening rivulets. The rear bumper bar is hanging at an odd angle, held precariously in place by a series of plastic shopping bags hastily knotted together. Shane is leaning forward, hands gripping the steering wheel, his head resting between them.

"Don't ask," he rasps. "I think I've died and gone to hell." He lifts his head and looks beseechingly at her. Despair and misery are etched on his face, streaked with dust that has stuck to the rotten potato slime, globules of it in his hair; wet patches of it all over his shirt. "And if I'm in hell, what are you doing here?" His shoulders sink as he rests his head once again on the steering wheel. Each exhalation is a torturous guttural groan of anguish. Kelsie wants to comfort him and leans forward to place a hand on his head, but the stench overwhelms her. She pulls back, instead moving her hand to cover her nose and mouth.

"Don't move." As if he would or could. "I'll be back. I'm going to get Greg."

\* \* \*

Greg is cowering behind the gum trees when Kelsie parks Sally's car. She has seen him as she pulls in but of course he doesn't recognise her. She climbs out and calls to him in a stage whisper.

"Greg. Greg. It's me."

"Where's Shane? I thought he was collecting me." Greg creeps towards her and slinks into the passenger seat. The expression on her face is unreadable.

"What's happened? Did the Arsehole catch you? I've been worried shitless!" She backs out without a word and drives silently back towards the truck stop. There is absolutely nothing she can say that will prepare him for the cataclysmic calamity awaiting them.

His fears and her silence fuelling the panic hormones racing between brain and mouth, he blabbers, "I knew you'd get caught. Why didn't Shane answer his bloody phone? Was Andy pissed off? I bet he was. He took off from the pub in a right old shit! I heard him spinning gravel and revving the hell out of his car from the back of the pub. And you should have heard the bar afterwards. The shouting, laughing and hullaballoo. I saw that big fat barmaid; Jesus what an arse. She was standing outside and talking on her phone for ages, carrying on, pissing herself laughing; and then she got into a beat-up old Holden and drove off. Jesus Kelsie, why aren't you saying anything? Where's Shane?"

She pulls up behind Valerie. Shane is as she left him but no longer making any noise. He raises his head to look forlornly at his brother. Greg repeats Kelsie's circling of the car.

"Holy bloody hell! *Jeeesars!*" He starts to laugh nervously, small incredulous chuckles escaping as he runs his hands over his head, pacing backwards and forwards and gagging at the stink. "Christ mate, I wouldn't want to be explaining *this* to Milton." It is Kelsie that brings him back to the immediate disaster.

"So where do we go from here? And it might be worth asking your brother if he is okay?"

"You alright Shane?" Shane nods.

"Do we drive away as is?" Kelsie again. "Find a car wash?" Greg looks at her in complete disbelief. What a stupid bloody question.

"Find a tip more like. Nup. We need to get the bulk of that shit," he pauses, "literally," and waves his hands in the air; "out of the seats," he circles the car yet again. "And the floor." He shakes his head; "and the roof." Attempting to lift the boot, he discovers the emergency measures Shane has put in place to secure the bumper. He nudges it with his foot and turns to Kelsie.

"What's Sal got in her car?"

A dustpan and brush, a four-litre container of water, several supermarket plastic bags, each tied neatly in a loose knot, a pair of old paint-stained but neatly folded bib and brace overalls, a length of light rope, a bag full of clean cotton rags, and a travel blanket and car cleaning kit. The last two obviously gifts, are found in the boot. A box of tissues, a packet of baby wipes, two music CDs and the registration and vehicle instruction manual folder are found in the glove box. Valerie's glove box provides an old metropolitan street directory, tissues and a small leopard skin case containing a black suspender belt, black mesh stockings, a diamante G string and long drop sparkling clip-on earrings. Kelsie discovers these and tucks the case discretely back into its hiding place.

"You up to removing the shit outta the car?" Greg offhandedly questions Shane. "Given you're already covered in it. I don't see why we need to contaminate ourselves." Shane has finally stepped out of Valerie and is pacing backwards and forwards between the two cars, breathing deeply and exhaling loudly.

"Oh Gawd. All of a sudden, I'm feeling like shit. I'm sick. Oh Christ; I am really, *really* sick" Sitting down heavily onto the graded mound of dirt to the side of the road, he places his head between his knees in the anti-fainting posture.

"Herrrgghhh!" he vomits loudly. "Herrrgghhh!" Again. He groans. Kelsie takes a cotton rag from Sal's boot, and dowsing it with water, hands it to him.

"Herrrgghhh!"

Greg turns away. Anyone vomiting seriously unsettles him and the stink of sheep shit, chicken shit, rotten pota- toes and rotten tomatoes mixed with the escalating stink of Shane's vomit is more than he needs to trigger a reac- tion. He gags and holds his breath, then walks away slowly, heading north up the highway. His hands clasped behind his head, he looks intently at the horizon and takes deep, measured breaths.

Kelsie takes the damp cloth from Shane and holds it to his forehead as she strokes his back; compassion finally transcending her revulsion at his physical dilemma.

"Oh, you poor, poor thing." She looks briefly at the pool of vomit between his feet and can make out fragments of hotdog, beetroot and fried egg as well as masticated cheese and bread slime.

"I think that Super dog has given you food poisoning," she says.

"Herrrgghhh!" There are no more projectile fluids coming from Shane as he leans forward staring intently into the roadside gravel. "Herrrgghhh!" He is now dry-retching, long slimy strands of saliva trailing from his gaping mouth. He manages to gasp and groan hysterically in between each diabolical gastric contraction.

"Herrrgghhh! Oh god! Oh fuck," he groans. "I wish that ... Herrrgghhh ... crazy bastard ... Herrrgghhh... had killed me. Now I've ... Herrrgghhh ... shit myself." Greg flings his hands in the air.

"Oh Jesus. That's *all* we need." He stalks off along the highway, then stands, hands on hips, gazing out across the pastures, stamping his feet, and struggling to suppress his escalating urge to throw up. He recognises the lights of a farmhouse blinking in the distance and focusses on them. At that precise moment he is rocked by the shattering noise and violent gusts of wind as an enormous milk tanker roars past them. Looking back, he can see that Kelsie has the baby wipes in her hands and is now sitting next to Shane, cradling his head in her lap as she gently wipes his brow and his hair, his cheeks, his closed eyes, his hands and his arms, a little mound of discarded wipes growing beside her. She pauses to look at Greg, now facing her and looking back in disgust at the pitiful sight before him.

"*Listen arsehole*," she yells; "This is *not about* you. Your brother is seriously ill. God knows what else happened to him back there. I think he's in shock. Get Valerie sorted so that we can get the fuck out of here."

# Chapter 5

Saturday morning.

Milton walks slowly around his beloved Valerie, his hands tucked into each of the back pockets of his bum-hugging, steam-pressed jeans, a cream lamb's wool jumper draped casually around his neck over a purple long-sleeved silk shirt. His casual sophistication in striking contrast to the atrocity that sits in silent humility and desolation before him.

"Oh Valerie, you poor dear, what have they done to you?" He is beyond anger or outrage; his initial shock transmuted to a state of wide-eyed disbelief. Greg and Shane are standing several paces back, bracing themselves, immersed in a mutual cloud of guilt and shame. They both look ill, though only Shane truly qualifying. He is still physically frail in the aftermath of the Super Dog explosions of the night before and is now wearing a lady's faded old chenille dressing gown over a pair of oversized ladies track pants secured at the waist by a pair of black tights. He is feigning confidence, but is obviously embarrassed and humiliated in this emergency attire on the back of his primary participation in the catastrophe that has brought them all together. They had agreed not to attempt to clean the shit and stink from Valerie, believing it needs a measured professional approach, but also so that Milton can actually see the degree of desecration inflicted upon his treasure by the protagonist in last night's mission. No one could have predicted Andy's massively aggressive and manic response.

They are standing on the back lawn of Kelsie's Nonna's house, where Valerie has been parked to hide her shameful condition from the prying eyes of neighbours and passersby. The pong emanating from her interior far surpasses that of a wheelie bin. Both Kelsie and her grandmother are absenting themselves from the vehicle inspection. They checked it out together earlier, so shocked by the appalling spectacle that they were rendered speechless, although Nonna managed a few clucks and winces.

With the confidence, competence, and common sense that Milton had acknowledged in her, Kelsie had taken control of the previous evening's debacle. She had been seriously concerned for Shane's welfare and had made that the priority, deciding instinctively to take him to her grandmother, who would know what to do, and who lived less than half an hour away. He had been transported in the laidback front passenger seat of Sally's car after his poo-filled trousers and potato-slimed shirt had been removed.

Greg reluctantly and shamefacedly followed Valerie, his head and arms poking through the holes he had made in the oversized unused black plastic bin liner salvaged from an empty garbage bin in the truck bay. He had been thankful for the fresh air blowing across his face, the car roof unable to be raised, so that Valerie's powerful stench was mostly detected in her wake, echoing the excretal odours that follow stock trucks up and down the very same highway. The last of the cleaning rags had protected his hands from the slimed steering wheel, as black plastic flapped and fluttered hysterically in his ears. It had been a driving experience he would long remember.

He had seriously disgraced himself with Kelsie. Instructed to help his brother clean up with the water and rags from Sal's car, he had lain Shane face down and spreadeagled across the bonnet, his brother's poor bare bum shining in the moonlight as he dowsed him with splashes of cold water, just as one might in a tokenistic attempt to put out a fire, turning his head away in disgust with each thrust of the water container. Kelsie had finally lost it and taken over, but not before pushing him out onto the highway and yelling at him to get Sal's car ready.

After wiping him down with rags she'd helped Shane into Sally's overalls, securing them with the length of rope around his waist after they slid to his ankles twice, indicating he was too weak and distracted to continually hold them up. He had by then been managing longer periods of silence, breathing less heavily between occasional spasms of dry retching. Tortured groans had punctuated his efforts to cooperate with her as she wrapped him in the blanket and lowered him into Sally's car. Thankfully, after the initial violent emptying of his bowels, his body's response to the Super Dog poisoning had remained at the oral end.

Greg had scoured the roadside to find a sturdy stick with which to poke Shane's sodden stinking clothes into one of the supermarket plastic bags before dropping them into the truck bay's bin. He completely overlooked the soiled runners, and these would be likewise tossed into the bin by a disdainfully disgusted matron the very next morning. Despite being wrapped in the travel blanket, Shane had continued to shiver violently all the way to Nonna's house. Kelsie had been unsure how much of this was due to the food poisoning, the shock of his encounter with Andy, or his brother's callous incompetence.

After the confusing babble describing the evening's outcome late the previous night, Milton had been seriously concerned for the welfare of his troika of slaves. He'd sent them on this mission; and whatever the outcomes, he was responsible! Driving Brian's 4WD Toyota to collect him from the airport, they had travelled directly down the freeway to Nonna's house.

Brian, just now returning from a diversionary trip to the supermarket for cigarettes, lets himself through the side gate and joins him. He is shorter and stockier than his lover, with a casual confidence that sits companionably with his almost blatantly understated casual attire. Hands tucked into side pockets, his thumbs pointing at each other over his unironed, faded denim jeans, he walks slowly around Valerie, silently taking in the details of the devastation; his expression unreadable. At last, he speaks.

"*Shiiiiiiit! Holy Fucking Christ*." He stops, bends over to look closer at the sheep pellets and chicken manure on the back seats, straightens up and says to no one in particular. "Now that was one seriously angry fuckhead."

He looks at Milton. Milton looks back at him. Each stares intently and knowingly into the other's eyes. Shane and Greg brace themselves; looking to each other for courage, as one wishing they could disappear. Brian and Milton slowly smile. Smiles turn into grins. Their shoulders begin to quiver. Each is holding his breath with the occasional nasal snort until they climax together in one loud cacophony of laughter. Milton now bent over with his hands on his hips, laughs hysterically into the lawn. Brian is holding his hands to the sides of his head and turns away, a visual separation needed to manage his mirth. Kelsie and her grandmother bustle out onto the verandah to see what the ruckus is about. They smile, look at each other, and begin to giggle nervously. Greg laughs hesitantly but Shane is only able to manage a cautiously nervous grin.

"Phew", gasps Brian, as he regains control. "Looks like my brother-in-law is a tad pissed off," he chuckles. "And what could he possibly do after a rage like that to finish off his day, screw the heads off some chooks or send shotgun blasts through a few road signs?" Greg, his relief and confidence returning, emits his own guttural giggle.

"Yeah," he drawls, "Well I have a pretty good idea." Another giggle. "Guess who else had the Super Dog for his counter meal." He pauses for dramatic effect. "At best he finished up on the dunny with a bucket between his knees. Although I rather hope he didn't have time to drop his dacks and he's still lying in it all on his back lawn." They all start laughing again, until Nonna ushers them inside.

Milton enthusiastically savours her Italian brewed coffee and semolina orange cake, celebrating both her hospitality and her company. She, likewise, takes an immediate fancy to him. Shane relaxes enough to describe his meeting with Andy. Kelsie stands behind him, her hands resting on his shoulders when not stroking his hair, intermittently kissing him gently on the top of his head. Beneath the humour surrounding his confrontation with Andy, everyone present recognises that he had been seriously threatened and lucky to escape comparatively unharmed.

"Let's get you some clothes," interrupts Brian. "I'm sure Nonna here would like hers back."

Nonna grins. "Oh, they just be me old ones. I been saving them to dress up the scare crow, but they look better on this young man." She pats Shane amiably on the shoulder. "You can keep them if you like." She laughs heartily, her huge breasts shaking beneath her old-fashioned wrap around apron.

"Stop teasing him Nonna," laughs Kelsie. "Greg come help me get Shane some gear from Target. How's your credit card?"

"Let me," says Brian, and all three stroll out to his car. Shane leaves Nonna and Milton chatting in the kitchen and retires to the lounge room, turning on the TV to watch the end of Rage on the ABC. Usually the clown or comedian, he instinctively seeks solitude and mindless distractions.

By the time Brian, Kelsie and Greg return, Nonna and Milton have devised the solution to Valerie's cleanup. All while Milton had followed her around her vegetable garden hugging a plastic bucket to his chest, chuckling and clucking his praise as she filled it with capsicums, chillies, a zucchini, a butternut pumpkin, some runner beans and broad beans, and a bunch each of basil, Italian parsley and mint. She now bustles him over to the verandah where Brian and Greg are waiting, Kelsie having taken the shopping inside to Shane. Milton is relaxed and positively beaming.

"Nonna here has offered to clean up Valerie," and he bursts into laughter. "She and her neighbours want to share the manure and rotten vegies to add to the compost for their vegie gardens; and they'll also clean her up." He laughs again. "And she says her grandson can replace the bumper and polish up the paint work as a project with his panel beating apprenticeship."

"Ah he's a good boy," beams Nonna. "He'll do a good job. You'll see. And me and Katerina next door, we'll have your car back good as new. We Italian ladies, we know how to clean. We're not afraid to get dirty. We have our hands in compost and shit every day." Her great breasts shake violently as she laughs robustly yet again; meanwhile waddling over to the room at the end of her verandah. She can be heard rattling around inside and emerges with a hessian bag for the vegies and a cardboard box filled with jars.

"For Brian," she grins in his direction. "My passata sauce, some pickles and a bottle a my wine. You are the chef; but you needa some proper Italian food, like I make."

\* \* \*

Kelsie and Shane remain with Sally's car at Nonna's, giving into her insistence that they stay at least till the end of the weekend. Brian and Milton drive Greg home, arriving back at the hotel shortly after midday. Brian holds his sister firmly in a silent embrace as she clings to him, crying gently into his shirt.

"It's okay Sal. It's over. You're going to be fine. You're safe. The boys are safe." She pulls away, sniffs loudly, and wipes her eyes with the backs of her hands.

"I don't know where that came from. I was just fine till you walked in the door." Milton turns away, dabs at his eyes with his neatly folded handkerchief, before flapping it open and loudly blowing his nose. He recovers his composure by fluffing around in the kitchenette to locate wine glasses. Sally and Brian smile at each other.

"Well, I believe a celebration is in order." Milton pops the cork on the bottle of bubbly that he'd placed in the fridge in anticipation of this very moment. He fills three flutes well beyond the levels normally considered appropriate and laughs as he sees both Sal and Brian raise their eyebrows in mock disdain at him.

"Oh, the three fingers from the top is for pooftas. If I want a drink, I want a proper drink." He laughs. "And I want a bloody drink." He sips from the top of his glass and then raises it. "Here's to you Sal." He takes another, longer sip. "And here's to Valerie. Neither of you deserve the shit that arsehole has thrown at you."

"I'm so sorry," says Sally.

"Well don't be. It wasn't your fault. It was nobody's fault. At least now we know what we're up against." He looks across at Brian as they all lower themselves into chairs; Brian and Sally sharing the settee.

"We've been talking on our drive back," says Brian. "It's definitely too dangerous for you to come to Grannie's house with us. I wouldn't want the boys there either; not that I worry about Andy harming them. I just don't want them to be present if he decides to come visiting."

Milton joins in. "We think it would be a good idea if you and the boys go away for a while. I'm sure you can take them out of school for a week." They begin talking in tandem, each filling in the gaps or taking up where the other leaves off.

"We think it would be best if you tell them both as soon as possible. In fact tomorrow would be a good idea."

"We can take them out of school and go sailing. I'm sure we can wangle it with their housemaster. Then bring them back here."

"In fact, under the circumstances, we could just collect them and take you all right away for a bit."

"What about Dave's dad's shack up the coast?" Brian is directing his question to Milton. "Where is that? Lancelin?"

"Hold on fellas. Slow down." Sally laughs at them both. "Mat and Benjie are no longer little kids. Yes, I need to let them know, and yes, I want to shield them from any fallout from their father; but they need to decide what is best for themselves. They might have things planned that they don't want to miss."

"Oops. Sorry," says Milton. "We got carried away. I think we might have run off the page." He shrugs an apology. "But Sal, we are both so pleased you have left; we just want to whisk you away. Away from any more trouble, away from any threats from that Arsehole. Perhaps we could look at some priorities and options, what's preferable and what's possible, and let the boys have a choice." He looks at Brian and then back to Sally. "And you too of course, Sal. What is it that you most want for yourself right now?"

She sits in silence, thinking, sipping on her drink, thinking some more, struggling to define what she is feeling, but knowing that until she does, she'll be unable to make any plans or decisions.

"I need time. I can't just run away. I need to know that Shane and Greg and Kelsie are alright. I know it has been worse for them than you're telling me right now. I knew from your questions last night Milton, not to mention the haste in which you raced off to rescue them this morning, that something serious had happened." She pauses. They each allow her time to respond without interruption.

"I need to speak to them and have that settled, before I see the boys." She takes a contemplative sip of her wine. "I need to get some clothes. And I need to get out of here, into some fresh air and sunshine. I've been stuck in air-conditioned rooms for over a fortnight." She laughs. "But first I need to have lunch. Take me somewhere with trees and water and birds and no traffic and no people and top food."

"Right," says Brian. "Food before or after clothes shopping? You look fine by the way, as long as you don't wish to go nightclubbing. But then we could always find you something flashy to wear, couldn't we, Milton?" He stands and slaps his lover on the shoulder. "Let's go. I know just the place."

* * *

Less than half an hour later they are strolling along a bush path meandering through eucalypt trees and wildflowers to a shelter on the edge of native forest in King's Park, overlooking the Swan River. Brian is carrying three folding chairs and a collapsed camping table, Sally a picnic basket, and Milton trails behind with an esky while chatting animatedly to someone on his mobile phone. Brian meanwhile is doing his best to distract Sally from what is unfolding. He sits her to the side and deftly assembles the small table, draping it in a white linen tablecloth. He sets it with three wine glasses, stainless steel cutlery, white china dinnerware and white linen napkins. He laughs at her stunned expression as she watches each item being extracted from the basket and placed ceremoniously on the table.

"Milton," he says. "Just can't help himself. Always has his fine dining kit on hand in the boot of my car. Chairs, table, basket, and esky. He hates roughing it... anywhere; and refuses categorically to camp out. If there's no bed, toilet and shower on hand he will not party!"

"Are you talking about me?" Milton glides into the shelter and extracts a bottle of Pinot Noir and another of soda water from his esky. "I hope there are water glasses in that basket as well." He clucks disdainfully when it becomes evident that there isn't. Brian brandishes three stainless steel pannikins and grins back mischievously.

"Suck it up sister. You'll just have to drink your soda from these; unless you want to dilute your *chilled* pinot with it."

"Don't be a boorish ass," quips Milton with mock indignation. "You know I only drink chilled Pinot in spring and summer, and the soda is so that we don't get too pissed; or are you offering to be driver Bob?"

"I'm sure you can call in a slave to drive us back if need be," says Brian as he looks at his watch and pulls a packet of cigarettes from his pocket.

"Ah, eating El fresco in the bush means I can have a smoke, and I'm seriously nicotine deprived at this minute. Pour us a drink will you Millie. How much longer before lunch arrives?"

Sally sips on her soda water and watches wide eyed as two young women dressed in tailored black and white checked trousers, white shirts, black neck kerchiefs, and short black aprons walk towards them from the car park, each with a padded carry bag. They smile and nod at Milton, placing their cargo on the ground, and with confidence, care and panache, place a mini smorgasbord on the table. They hand Sally a plate and serve her silver service style from each selection. She is at first speechless and then effervescently happy and playful, embracing the pantomime and immersing herself in it.

Later as they are sipping on long black coffees, poured with understated ceremony from a stainless-steel thermos into the hastily drained pannikins, picking through an immodest selection of chocolate truffles and petit fours, Sally badgers her brother and brother-in-law into confessing how they had performed this catering miracle. The young women have already packed up and left them to their afternoon.

"We're both in the biz, Sal. We each have friends in restaurants and eateries who can rustle up a feast in minutes. Milton has his team of slaves who just love the opportunity to dress up and do something different or outrageous. Catering in unusual places and at short notice is not as hard as it might appear."

"You should see some of the events, people and places I have been asked to cater to," croons Milton, now noticeably affected by his third glass of Pinot. "Fancy dress and cross-dressing cocktail parties," he giggles, "Or cock something on a catamaran cruising the Swan River; an all-time favourite for some people we know. Well, we know of them, even if we don't actually know them; if you know what I mean." He giggles yet again.

Sally laughs. An unprecedented intimacy is growing between them, as they envelop her in their mutual love and protection. She suspects the change is more in herself than the two men sitting before her. Leaving Andy, immersing herself in the freedom this gives her, allows her to relax the guards that have always hovered over her feelings and conversations.

"There are many facets to our culture Sal," Brian explains; she knowing instinctively that he is referring to the gay community in which he and Milton live and work.

"It's a long, long way from where we grew up; and of course, where you've always lived. You'll see. But like life anywhere, it's what you make it. It can be exciting, dull, dangerous, tedious, entertaining, and fun. It has its good side. It has its dark side. And as I tell Matt and Benjie, life is what it is, depending on the choices we make. And we all, regardless of opportunities, have choices. Even no choice is a choice."

She reflects on this last statement. Is he directing it at her? He goes nowhere with it, lighting up another cigarette as Milton begins packing up the last of their picnic. Even no choice is a choice. What of the life choices she has made? How many did she allow others to make for her? Or were all her choices ultimately her own? Can she, should she, be making choices for herself and the boys now, before understanding the challenges ahead? It's all just too hard.

"Come on Sal," says Brian as he helps her out of her chair. "One step at a time, one day at a time. Let's get you back to your hotel. And I'm driving, Millie. You're pissed!"

# Chapter 6

Early Saturday morning

His head feels ready to explode. At last the dogs have stopped whining. Insects are exploring and feasting on his arms, his legs, and his buttocks. The piercing scream of mosquitoes defines their perpetual frenzied orbit around his head. Andy attempts to open his eyes. Only one cooperates. He is lying belly down on the back verandah dressed only in his shirt. He can just make out the avenue of gum trees down his driveway, as they stand in silent silhouette against the predawn glow gently proclaiming a new day. Rolling tentatively and painfully onto his side, swatting feebly at the mozzies, and shaking his head ever so gently, he tries to muster the energy and concentration to remember what has brought him here. Where are his clothes? Why has he been sleeping on the concrete? What day is this? Why does everything hurt? Has he been beaten up? Where is Sal?

Oh fuck! His tongue is swollen, completely dry and crusty. He rolls it around, an insane image invading his emerging consciousness of a scaly bobtail lizard's head wedged in his mouth. He tries in vain to rustle up some saliva. Sliding his hand in bewilderment over the back of his head he finds clumps of hair knotted and stuck together with assorted debris. One by one he identifies the pieces of garden detritus in it. A broken leaf, some dried grass, and several slivers of wood chips. He finds also that he has a very tender swelling on his right cheekbone and a large hard lump above his right eyebrow. His right eye is swollen shut. There are crumbs in the bristles around his mouth. Plucking some free to squint at them through his one bleary eye, he discovers they are crystals of dried blood. Cautiously scratching away the blood trail that stretches to his cheekbone he finds a crusty crater too painful to explore any further.

Absent-mindedly dropping his hand to release the tension he feels around his genitals, he finds his penis glued in a tangle of pubic hairs, pointing neither up nor down, but in an awkward limp curl to the side. He gently releases it and decides not to investigate the sorry state he knows instinctively is defining his nether regions, his buttocks seemingly glued together. Every muscle protests as he raises himself first on hands and knees; using the verandah post as a prop to bring himself dizzily and precariously to his feet. He is seriously lightheaded, nauseous, and extremely weak. Clinging feebly to the post, he knows this is not just a hangover. He is grievously ill.

One of the kelpie dogs begins straining on his chain and flings Andy's wet and stained jeans from side to side in a playful frenzy as if trying to show his owner where to find his clothes. Memories come filtering back. He recalls turning on the garden hose, intent on washing his arse, having removed both his jeans and his boots after soiling them during waves of explosive vomiting and diarrhoea. He had skidded and slipped drunkenly on the wet and slimy smooth concrete, falling heavily onto his right shoulder, and hitting his head on an unopened can of dog food. Fortunately, this had been on the rounded edge and the can had been propelled along the verandah, rolling gleefully until captured by a cluster of abandoned farm footwear near the back door.

Still in the grip of his Super Dog food poisoning, he had continued vomiting, then dry retching violently. He remembers the humiliation of trying to clamp his bum cheeks shut and feeling warm trickles of slimy shit lubricating his crack and the back of his thighs with each gut-wrenching expulsion. Stunned, bleeding and in pain; from both his fall and the continuing stomach cramps, he had surrendered, helpless and defeated. He had then drifted between semi-consciousness, alcohol-induced paranoid hallucinations and horrendous nightmares, kindled and punctuated by the intermittent cacophony of howling dogs.

He is becoming progressively aware of the malodorous combination of smells threatening to overwhelm him. Putrescent dog food, seriously soiled dog bedding; rank unwashed dog hair; together with fresh and ageing dog shit. Overriding it all is the overpowering stench emanating from what appears to be desiccating pools of his own vomit and shit. He is thankful at least that his stomach is empty, or he might throw up at the sight and stink of it all.

He leans down to retrieve the hose and with great care and apprehension takes the four shaky steps needed to reach the tap. It appears to be still turned on. Turning it backwards and forwards in futile cycles of desperation, his panic escalating, he comes to the alarming realisation that there is no water. What the fuck? The tank must be empty. Why hasn't the automatic pump kicked in and refilled it? Christ he's thirsty. He has to have a drink. He has to have a shower. He needs water. Oh, Jesus fucking Christ? He must be back in his nightmare.

Sitting heavily onto the mess of old blankets littering the space between each of the kelpies' detention areas, he reaches desolately for one of their water buckets; only to discover that both are empty. The dogs in their previous night's panic and distress have tipped them over, wetting themselves and their bedding. They are now becoming increasingly excited at what seems to be an uncharacteristic show of affection from their master. Frantically wagging their tails and swinging their bodies side to side, they nuzzle Andy in the face and under his arms, licking the back of his neck and sniffing enthusiastically at his crotch and his bum.

He pushes them away, trying to scream abuse at them, but managing only to rasp out a low guttural roar. His jaw aches; his tongue, still stiff, dried out and inoperable. Groaning in frustration as the dogs fail to let up, their chains threatening to entangle him; he rolls despairingly out onto the lawn. It is a flood with water that has run free from the hose in the preceding hours.

Exhausted, he lies there on his stomach, distress and desolation overtaking him. Gradually the revitalising coolness of the swamp he has unknowingly created begins to sooth him and he turns to rest first one cheek and then the other in the waterlogged cushion of grass. His mouth so dry, he purses his lips painfully and sucks loudly on the water. Resting between each swallow, he is surprised at how cool and fresh it tastes. He waits tentatively to see if each small mouthful will bounce straight back out when it hits his stomach. They stay. The nausea eases; the vomiting doesn't return. Slowly sating his thirst, and then loudly, defiantly, drinking his fill; he pauses several times to release a putrid belch. With his one functioning eye closed in comparative relief, ecstasy even; he rests, trying to bring his mind to a place of clarity where he might assess his immediate physical predicament.

His oasis experience has revived him enough to roll painfully onto his back. He surrenders to exhaustion, resting motionless in the cool comfort of the soggy lawn. It calms him. He feels a little confidence returning and almost feels able to squeeze out a short morning fart. But with the memories of failing anal retention returning in humiliating waves, he decides against it; continuing to lie there spread-eagled, gazing through one bleary eye at the early morning sky. There are few stars, a gentle illumination unfolding.

Matching the beginning of this new day, it slowly begins to dawn on him just how much shit, some of it literally, he has put himself in. No water. Bugger all clean clothes. No laundry has been done since Sally went to hospital. And not only is the house a stinking neglected domestic mess, he now remembers how he had trashed it, his rage overtaking his sanity as he transformed it into a demolition disaster area. And ... there is no Sal.

He revisits his two meetings with her emissaries. Or were they one? They had both looked the bloody same. Or maybe one was dressed differently. Shamed and humiliated by the first in front of the whole bar at the pub. Violently brought to the ground with a totally unexpected head tackle by the second; they had seriously contributed to his current ruination. Who were they? The fuckin' little shits! Who did they *think* they were? Fuck 'em! But this trigger-happy return to rage immediately transforms into a self-indulgent melancholy. He knows with absolute certainty Sally will not be coming home.

So long has he taken her for granted; assuming without thinking, that she will somehow always be there. His. Like his property and house and inheritance. She has never complained, at his choices, his behaviours, his habits, his absences. She has always just got on with the daily routines, both business and domestic, keeping him informed and fed and comfortable, whilst retreating deeper and deeper into her blank emotionless silences. He has no idea what goes on inside her head. But then he's never actually thought about it.

His memory of how their life together started has become distorted by the early dismissal of his part in it, and the now long-forgotten feelings of guilt. He is, as he has always been, incapable of introspection, living each day as it comes, following the seasonal and social patterns that have defined his adult life. He lies there in self-indulgent, arrogant ignorance; oblivious to the role he has played in Sally's long-term withdrawal. If he could muster a fleeting vestige of humility he might recognise the compounding consequences of his selfishness, bullying and neglect; culminating in her silently, passively, just not stepping off the bus.

He realizes, that for the first time ever, he is to be on his own, responsible for himself. First his mother and then Sal have cleaned his house, kept him fed, laundered his clothes, tidied up after him, cleaned his car, laid out his sports clothes, collected them and miscellaneous work clothes from where he's abandoned them to have them washed and pressed ready for when he next needs them.

Sal has been his business partner, managing the banking and finances, paying the bills, organising deliveries to the fruit and vegetable markets, managing private orders, sending out the invoices, helping with planting and harvesting, feeding workers, driving to town on errands, feeding orphaned lambs or calves. The enormity of the difference her absence will make to his ability to manage the farm, indeed just keep it operating, is slowly evolving. A storm of panic is brewing. He surrenders. A melancholy tear rolls tentatively down each cheek.

After Shane had sped off down the driveway in the Volvo Sports the night before, Andy had immediately searched for his shotgun. Finding the barrel and splintered remnants of the stock scattered in the driveway, he had stormed into the house in an escalating rage. Knowing he hadn't replenished the beer normally stocked in his fridge, he had grabbed the bottle of rum he kept stashed in an old cowboy boot in the bottom of his wardrobe. This secret reserve of alcohol sustaining the routine of a nightly drinking finale, taking a couple of swigs to lubricate his final slide into slumber.

He had taken long slugs of rum between guttural inhalations and raucous snorts as he'd scanned each room; gradually recognising what had been removed. Her laptop computer and sewing machine, the photo albums, her mother's fancy fucking glass and china. He'd kicked an abandoned suitcase in the hallway and on further investigation, discovered the wardrobe and chest of drawers in her bedroom still held her clothes. Her framed photos, books, and girly nick-knacks appeared also to have been untouched. He couldn't specifically identify anything missing because he'd never been in there nor had any interest in doing so. Just as she'd never been in their so-called marital bed.

Draining the last of the rum from the bottle, he'd hurled it in a wave of hysterical fury through Sally's bedroom window, the violent crashing and smashing of glass further inflaming this tumultuous tantrum. He'd staggered to his ute to grab a new bottle of rum from the six-pack purchased on his trip to town, tearing off the screw top lid and guzzling it greedily. His hysteria had escalated until he completely lost himself in a frenzy of destruction, sweeping everything off every surface, emptying cupboards and drawers, strewing their contents across the floor, kicking clothes, boxes, books into the walls. He had advanced next to her sewing room, then the lounge room and finally the kitchen. All the while slugging on the rum and screaming his rage mantra, "Bitch. Bitch. You fuckin' bitch." It was during his kitchen rampage that he'd been abruptly interrupted by the sudden onset of nausea and gut cramp. He had only just managed to scramble drunkenly through the debris to the back verandah before collapsing into a heaving, vomiting, and excreting mess.

Regaining some strength, but still unsteady and nauseous, Andy now stands to wobble his way down the garden path to the side gate, intent on discovering why the automatic pump has not refilled the gravitational storage tank towering over the rear end of the car port. He hastily retreats in agony from the first unsteady steps off the concrete, as sharp stones dig viciously into his bare feet. Wincing, limping and cursing his way back to the verandah, he leans heavily against the wall for support and pulls on a pair of black rubber boots. He's exhausted. His head is throbbing. He needs to sleep. But he needs a shower. He needs water.

His sodden, filthy, checked shirt clings untidily to his lean body, just covering his naked crotch and buttocks. His streaked, hairy, and well-muscled legs stick out farcically above the rubber boots as he leans against the house yard fence, peering through his one open eye up to the tank and then down to the electric pump at its base. He can see nothing different. He looks up, feels dizzy, steadies himself, and looks down; repeating this cycle three times before recognising the problem. The door to the small box under the tank stand is hanging by one hinge. It has split, obviously damaged by something hitting it with substantial force. On the ground less than a metre away, the splintered remains of his shotgun solve the mystery .

"Aw fuckin' hell, ya fuckin' bastard." He realises that Shanes bungled hammer throw had catapulted the shotgun onto the master switch for the electric pump. He will have to get the petrol firefighting pump from the farm shed and connect it to the water main bringing water from the house dam.

He swoons and groans at the thought of the effort this entails as he wobbles unsteadily over to his farm ute. The driver-side door is hanging open, the keys still in the ignition. Lowering himself into the seat he hastily readjusts his posture, grappling frantically for a discarded jacket to protect his bare arse, the exposed wires on the worn seat cover threatening to ensnare his testicles. He turns the ignition key. There is an elongated decelerating moan and then nothing.

"Aw, Jesus fucking Christ. Fuck! Fucking fuck!" He leans his head in defeat against the steering wheel. "Fucking fuck, fuck, fuck!" The battery is flat. The headlights were left on the previous night after illuminating the shed to locate and load his shotgun. He would beat his head in desperation against the steering wheel, but given the pain pulsating across his crown, and his rapidly diminishing capacity for raging, he changes his mind and leans back into the driver's seat. Resting his head instead against the headrest, he pushes his hands feebly into the steering wheel before sliding them limply to his sides. Exhaustion and despair overtake him.

A rhythmic wailing noise intrudes on his consciousness. He holds his breath and listens. It stops. This raucous noise is coming from him. He is howling; just like a great big kid. He swallows, groans and surrenders; releasing himself to waves upon waves of loud, open-mouthed howling as he hasn't done since he was eight years old, the day his grandfather died.

* * *

"Hey Andy; you okay mate?" Andy wakes groggily to the sound of Jim Kessel's voice and the gentle but firm pressure of a gnarled hand on his shoulder. The sun is now well into the sky and has been blazing down on him through the windscreen for at least an hour. He has cried himself back into an exhausted sleep. He still has the skull-splitting headache and is struggling to open his one functioning eye. He can just make out the great bulging bulk of his eighty-year-old neighbour hovering over him.

"Where's Sal? What's happened? Hey Janice; get over here will ya. Keep an eye on Andy for me while I check out the house." A stout woman in her mid-seventies waddles over with ageing, dysfunctional hips and peers in at him. She immediately notices the absence of his trousers and peers a little closer, gazing at the insignificant curl of a penis hanging limply between his spread-eagled legs; his bedraggled shirt gathered in untidy folds up around his waist. Andy squints back at her through his one eye and lets out a long-winded groan. Christ almighty, fucking Janice. The last person he wishes to see.

"My goodness Andy, you've got yourself into a right old mess." She leans forward and pulls his shirt gently down over his penis, tucking it in and giving his thigh a gentle pat. "Best you keep that covered for now matey; even if you are in the habit of showing it around." She releases a quietly cynical cackle. She and Jim have been neighbours to the Chesters since long before Andy was born. She knows the family history and most of their secrets. She and his mother had been friends and neighbours right up until Margaret died. She knows Andy only too well; holding him in barely concealed contempt; having been quietly observing his belligerent, narcissistic behaviours since his boyhood.

"Sal's not there." Jim rolls his ageing bulk back to the ute after releasing the dogs. He has unsuccessfully attempted to refill their water buckets but sees them lapping from puddles still remaining in the swamp now receding from Sally's garden.

"And her car's gone. The house is a bloody mess; never seen anything like it. Looks like vandals have been in and had a grand old time trashing the place. Only Andy's and the boys' bedrooms seem to be untouched. There's vomit and blood and shit on the back verandah; and Andy's boots and trousers. The whole back yard looks like it's been flooded."

He leans in towards Andy. "What happened mate? You able to talk yet?" Andy groans and looks out at them both. Janice has retreated, waiting silently to the side.

"Christ, that's one hell of a shiner you have there; and you could need a coupla stitches in that cut. Who belted ya? Here, stick ya arm around me shoulder and we'll get ya outta there." He helps Andy out and onto his feet.

"Jesus; you don't half stink. Nice boots though. Wouldna been my choice of footwear." He chuckles. "An' don't worry about Janice catchin' a look at John Thomas down there. She hasn't been interested in one of them for years! We'll get ya to the bathroom."

"No water;" croaks Andy. "Tank's empty."

He is beyond humiliation, surrendering to the relief that he is now immersed in the safety and supervision he needs, as he sits with a towel around his loins in the back of Jim and Janice's Subaru station wagon. His feet are sweltering in the fetid heat brewing in the base of his rubber boots. Jim doesn't let up for the four-minute drive to their old farmhouse on twenty acres just a kilometre down the road.

"We thought somethin' was up, didn't we Janice. Heard what, two, or was it three cars screamin' down ya driveway last night. And then a coupla gunshots. Thought ya were shootin' kangaroos. I said to Janice then, somethin's not right next door. Nup; it's just not right. We shoulda come and checked then Janice. I told ya. Yep, we should. It's not bein' nosy; just bein' good neighbours. And now Sal's missing. Who were they Andy? There had to be more than one of them."

"There was a bloke at the pub;" croaks Andy; "and a bloke waitin' for me when I got home. Someone drove Sal's car out as I got there."

"What? Kidnapped her in her own car? Jeesus. I told ya we should a come and checked Janice. I told ya. Who hit ya Andy? He whack ya with a cricket bat or somethin'? That's a hell of a crack on the scone you've had. Where do ya think they've taken Sal? Christ, I hope she's alright. Good woman Sal. Good woman." Andy winces as Jim bounces the Subaru over the cattle grid at the end of their driveway and pulls up at the back of their old unpainted timber farmhouse. It is framed on two sides by an enormous pine hedge that has long been neglected and now towers over them in feral disarray.

"I'll get Andy here to the bathroom Janice. You phone Rachel. See if she can come over. We need her to check him out. See if he needs ta go ta hospital. And then we'll ring the police."

"*Nooo*! Don't do that;" croaks Andy. "I have to work out what to do. I just need a shower, and some clothes, something for this fucking headache and a sleep."

\* \* \*

Following his lengthy shower, Rachel bustles in through the back door, gives Andy two heavy-duty painkillers and insists he drink the half-litre jug of a rehydration drink she has made from water, salt, and sugar. It tastes disgusting. He grumbles and gags on it.

"You're bloody dehydrated Andy, and hung over. Just bloody drink it and stop whingeing. You'll need to drink one of these every two hours for the rest of the day." Her dislike and impatience for this cousin thrice removed is obvious and she continues to harangue and boss him around as she checks the movement in his arms and painful right shoulder, measures his pulse and blood pressure and thrusts an old-fashioned thermometer less than gently into his mouth.

He admits to having been vomiting and having the shits, too afraid not to, in case a repeat episode befalls him. He doesn't own up to having slipped in his own excrement on his back verandah and cracking his cheek open on a can of Chum. He is allowing his attentive audience to believe Jim's earlier assumptions that he was mugged by a couple of intruders. He knows Sally hasn't been kidnapped, but there seems no point in correcting that assumption either.

He is dressed in a faded checked flannel shirt and an old pair of patched and fraying bib and brace overalls. Both belong to Jim who is a good ten centimetres taller and forty kilos heavier. He is not wearing underpants as Jim's bum is at least five sizes bigger and they won't stay on without the loop of elastic gleefully offered by Janice, and which Andy less than graciously declines. He really is a sight. His grossly oversized attire, his rapidly blackening, swollen, closed eye; three days' growth of greying whiskers and the two large butterfly sutures Rachel has improvised from some medical tape she pulled from the bowels of her first aid bag.

Together with his pale hangdog expression beneath his clean but uncombed spiky wild hair; all give the impression of a circus clown in an improvised costume. Behind his back Janice and Rachel look at each other and grin. Jim catches them and removes himself from the kitchen, mumbling into his double chins something about needing to find the battery charger. On his return, with Andy now sleeping off his malaise in the sunroom, he joins Rachel and

Janice for a cup of tea and a discussion as to Sally's possible whereabouts. Should they be calling the police?

"Andy does *not* want the Police called," says Jim. "At the same time he's not making any sense. He's been on an absolute bender while Sal's been in hospital. Maybe when she got home, she saw the mess and left. Andy said *someone* drove out in her car. Could it have been her? And he's just not sayin' like."

"Well we know that she was to catch the bus," says Rachel. "With Andy picking her up from the Pub. But we don't know that she actually got on the bus. Could she have caught the train to Perth to stay with her brother instead?" She looks across to Janet. "Have you got Brian's number? Look, Andy says he doesn't know where Sal is and we know he is a sly, conniving, lying bastard. But maybe he *is* telling the truth, though certainly not all of it."

Janet has returned to the table with an old Teledex. She slides the alphabet indicator slowly through the letters. "Now what's Brian's surname? Here he is."

"I say we try Brian first, maybe phone around," says Jim. "I don't reckon Andy has harmed Sal. The blood on the verandah I reckon is his. So, no point in going off half cocked an makin' a fool a ourselves. An' we don't wanna be makin' things more difficult for Sal. God knows she's had enough to deal with, without the Police huntin' her down, just to satisfy *our* curiosity. I'll get on ta Brian."

# Chapter 7

Sunday afternoon

It takes nearly three hours to get to Wangaree Shacks, the last twenty minutes careering along convoluted sandy tracks meandering through a sea of marram grass carpeting the broad stretch of coastal plain. Brian, in his element, a passionate 4WD driver, skilfully manoeuvres Tony Toyota, straddling the tufted central ridges, accelerating gleefully over loose boggy sand hills. Showing off as big brothers can. Sally defiantly not noticing as little sisters do, although she can't help grinning.

Her runners long discarded and dismissively tossed with their ankle socks to the back seat, she immediately heads for the ocean. A warm north-westerly breeze inspires the dune grasses to wave their welcome and she rejoices in its gentle ocean-scented caress, luxuriating in the sensory pleasure of warm soft sand pillowing her feet as she treks light-heartedly over the ridge down to the beach.

Pausing indecisively, Brian ponders whether to begin unloading the car, collect the key to their three-room shack from its assigned hiding place, or follow his sister as she celebrates her surrender to the healing allure of the ocean. There are absolutely no constraints on their time.

He chooses the latter. They have always been comfortable with each other, communicating easily within understood if undefined parameters. But these boundaries are now shifting, especially since he's begun to temper his angst towards Andy and his overprotectiveness of Sally and the boys, consciously listening to what she is saying, and not saying.

Hence their exodus from the hotel and the city this morning. He and Milton wanted her safely sequestered in a place they could trust to provide the security they believe she needs. Sally desperately wants to be free of constraints, interruptions, distractions and especially people; those she knows and those she doesn't. Anyone who might intentionally or idly question her. How she is, what she's doing, where she's staying, where she's from, does she have family, where are they, is she in town on business or for pleasure.

And she desperately needs to be in nature, in an unpolluted, uncontrived, minimally organized expanse of country, free of the frenetic movement of automobiles and foot travellers, free of the sounds and smells of the city. They are staying in the smallest of four well-spaced fishing shacks that have been in his sailing mate Dave's family for nearly fifty years, their coastal retreat from the rigours of wheat and sheep farming.

She sits rhythmically doodling and smoothing a slate of soft white sand between her spreadeagled legs, a bleached twig her stylus. She smiles affectionately as Brian joins her.

"Thank you. This is perfect. And for arranging for Matt and Benjie to visit last night, getting them back to college safely and on time." She laughs, "Wouldn't have happened if they'd had their way."

"Yeah, well, they could have stayed overnight if they hadn't been off to camp today. It's really very timely. Takes the pressure off. And Aunty Millie is more than happy to be the school's point of contact for the time being." He laughs. "He's never happier than when he can cluck around those he loves."

"I was surprised, but then not so, with their reactions to me leaving. They were actually really excited." She giggles animatedly. "Seeing it as an adventure, if not for them, then certainly for me. So many suggestions as to what I might do, where I might go, where we might live; and would this mean they can leave boarding school." She smooths her sand slate yet again, her mood now shifting, and plants her stylus firmly in its centre.

"I do need time to think all this through. I'm still reeling a bit. I mean,...." Speaking more to herself, "Have I finally done it?" She inhales and exhales slowly, deeply. Brian waits in cautious anticipation for where this conversation is going.

"It has taken so long," she sighs, releasing another long breath. "Should I.... Could I...... Could I have done this years ago?"

He stifles the cascade of questions jostling for an answer. Why, how, did she ever hook up with and marry Andy? Well, obviously, the latter because she was pregnant. But how in hell's name did she allow herself to have sex with him in the first place? She'd only just left school. What happened to her plans to go nursing? Why didn't she start her nursing training after the boys went to school? How did she share that house with Andy's mother for all those years? And then look after her when she'd had her stroke? It has so long tortured him. The questions must wait. Who will it serve to coerce answers from her now?

* * *

The key is where Dave told him, hanging from a cup hook screwed to the wooden verandah joist closest to the front door. Easy and convenient if not seriously secure, but anyone intent on entry wouldn't bother with a key anyway. The owners and periodic occupants of the shacks are all family, and friends of family. Its own trustworthy little community. Each sharing resources and skills so that they now have solar hot water and panels powering lights, LP gas for cooking and refrigeration, and septic systems replacing the original drum-lined long drops serving as outdoor dunnies. The basic, functional fittings inside and out enable unstructured holiday activities of boating, fishing, swimming, and luxuriating in laziness.

Each shack has a large rainwater tank as does the communal shed housing a couple of ancient dinghies with equally ancient outboard motors. Amassed in an ad hoc storage system are assorted fishing paraphernalia, a hodgepodge of salt-crusted tools, tins, ropes, sacks, bushwhacking implements, and a generous supply of mallee roots. Brian looks fondly at the smoke-smudged rocks defining the boundaries of the fire pit, remembering multi-family gatherings evolving well into starry nights, the last teetering stragglers sneaking off giggling guiltily as a new day dawned. The most recent technologically inspired installation has been a solar-powered satellite dish to boost mobile phone access.

He insists that Sally have the only bedroom with its antiquated double bed, while he bunks down in the kitchen/living room on one of the sleeping benches doubling as seating. The walls are lined and insulated, helping to minimise the entry of pestilential intruders and temper the thermal extremes of both summer and winter. All other fittings and furnishings generate a rustic simplicity ensuring housekeeping chores are minimised. Open shelved benches of untreated timber store kitchen utensils and perishable pantry items, all secured in clip-on lidded plastic boxes. A narrow floor-to-ceiling bookcase is haphazardly stocked with jigsaws, assorted board games, discarded dogeared magazines and an eclectic collection of books; mainly paperbacks, but some ancient, faded hardcovers that have likely not been opened in decades.

There's an old cast iron potbelly stove in one corner. The gas fridge decorated in a multiplicity of magnets resides in another. A large battered and scarred wooden table dominates the room. It is surrounded by a chaotic collection of kitchen and dining chairs that have found their final function and resting place. There is no television, no computer desk, no microwave or any other city-dwelling conveniences. The freestanding gas stove supplements the functions of the original old, enamelled wood stove that was installed outside. Encased in second or third-hand house bricks, it converts easily into a bush BBQ and has simmered countless flour drums of crabs and crayfish. Its wood ash dusty oven has baked hundreds of crunchy golden dampers perfect for plastering with butter and golden syrup.

The box of goodies from Nonna's garden and pantry has been supplemented by some premeditated shopping at the Farmers' Markets on their way out of the city. Brian gleefully selected his favourite healthy snack foods and the basic ingredients with which to whip up gourmet treats he hopes will tease and titillate his sister. He has long known her to be a competent and creative cook. He is planning to challenge her to a playful culinary contest. To these supplies he's added a cask each of top-shelf red and white wine, brandy for Sally, whisky for himself and their complimentary mixers.

Sally removes the tags and wrappings from the modest selection of clothes she'd tossed indifferently into a Kmart trolley, hovering around Brian as he creates a splendiferous antipasto smorgasbord and sets up faded director's chairs beside quaint tin tray folding tables around the fire pit. The trays are reminiscent of those their granny used long ago for TV dinners. He scavenges sticks, yellowing newspaper and crumbling fire starters from the depths of the shed to kindle the mood-lifting fire for their first evening of solitary celebrations. Just the two of them. How long has it been since they have had the luxury of each other's uninterrupted company?

"Oh the smell of percolating coffee. May I join you?" Brian turns half-heartedly in his chair to greet Dave's older brother Walter. He has only just returned from packing away the remnants of their meal, rehearsing in his mind opening gambits to encourage Sally to unburden herself, providing of course that she is ready.

"Wally! When did you arrive? We didn't see your car. Grab yourself a chair."

"Young Joey dropped me off yesterday for a few days. We've been flat strap and he's got himself some social distractions to chase up in the city." He laughs. "Nah. He doesn't need me tagging along. Arrived late, went fishing first thing and been snoozing all afternoon. I'll grab that chair. Hey. I've got a bottle of Windy Creek Liqueur Muscat. You interested in a nip or two?"

What could he say? "Sounds great. Wally, this is my sister Sally. Sal this is Walter. Wal or Wally for short." She nods a greeting.

"Nice to meet you," says Walter as he saunters back along the narrow track winding over a low grassy sandhill, muted moonlight lighting his way, although he could probably do it blindfolded.

"Sorry Sal. But he's a good bloke. Easy company. Lost his wife last year. Breast cancer. They'd been married twenty-seven years. Poor bugger." He leans forward to shift the blackened camping coffee pot to the side and toss another tangle of mallee root on the fire, a cascade of golden sparks exploding into the sky. "Could you get us another mug?"

By the time she is back with another pannikin Walter has returned with a folding chair under his arm, a wine bottle in one hand and clasping three shot glasses in the other, a finger in each. She sits back as the men dispense the wine and coffee, happily allowing them to take charge, becoming increasingly comfortable in being indulged and waited on. They cautiously swallow their steaming hot coffees, casually alternating with sips of the muscat, one drink complimenting the other. A soothing silence hovers between them. Walter is the first to speak.

"I never tire of visiting here, find any excuse to get over. Been doin' it now for nearly forty years." He turns to Sally. " I've got a coupla spare King George whiting in my fridge. I can drop them over tomorrow."

"Thank you," says Sally, "I haven't had one for years. I love them."

"Do you like fishing?"

"I've never really done any. Maybe. Our Dad had a little fishing boat, a dinghy. He loved to go fishing, but usually in the river estuaries. He would take us crabbing. I loved that; with scoop nets or drop nets off the jetty." She holds out her glass in response to Walter's raised bottle enquiry. Brian smiles and thrusts his glass forward.

"This is a very nice muscat. I could get a real taste for it." He grins.

"Nice little winery in the Swan Valley. Probably on your way home I reckon." Walter places the bottle on one of the tin tray tables and leans back in his chair, stretching his long legs before him.

"It's perfect for nights like this. Smelling and listening to the ocean. A proper mallee fire, enough of a breeze to keep the mozzies away, but without the need for a beanie". He pauses to sip on his muscat. "And good company."

Relieved at the ease with which Sally and Walter are warming to each other, neither asking the other intrusive questions, Brian is happy to defer any conversation around the questions he's been pondering. They can wait. He can see that his sister and her new friend are a comfort to each other, intuitively sensing the other's wounds, not needing to classify or quantify them. Everything at this moment is just as it needs to be.

As the evening progresses, conversation slowing, all three completely at ease with each other, Sally relaxes into a pattern of long, leisurely, rhythmic breathing, her mind slowed and empty. She surrenders to the warm evening breeze caressing her arms and shoulders. Gently stretching her neck she leans back in her chair to gaze at the stars. Walter, relaxing respectfully in her contemplative presence, rolls himself a cigarette and hands the tobacco pouch to Brian. They too are savouring the silence and balmy stillness of this night.

She stands and walks languorously along the sand dune track onto the beach, stopping at the waters' edge, feet sinking, settling slowly into the fluid sand, as the ebb and flow of each wave gently caresses her ankles. Brian and Wally stand in silence on the dune ridge watching over her protectively. They are intrigued, not worried. This is a mystical moment. She is completely immersed in it. They can sense it, knowing instinctively that words will diminish it.

Staring blankly out to sea, she eventually raises her hands to the sky, fingers wide and upturned palms her antennas as she gazes searchingly into the milky way. Eventually she turns, stepping dreamily back onto the soft dry beach sand, and removes first her t-shirt, then her jeans and underclothes. Oblivious to the presence of her brother and her new friend, she wades slowly back into the ocean until it caresses her belly, bathing the long horizontal scar, then sinks into the healing waters. *She lies back to float freely, surrendering to the rhythmic swell of the ocean, her body rising and falling in its loving embrace, safe in the womb of the universe.*

Brian feels two heavy tears run consecutively down his cheeks. He knows now, without a doubt, that his Sal has been carrying a wound deeper than he can ever comprehend, and for a very long time. Compassion and sorrow feel about to overwhelm him. Walter rests a hand gently on his shoulder, for just a moment, then gestures to the sand where they sit watching over her together. The ritual of sharing tobacco and smoking slowly rolled cigarettes, replacing conversation. For there is nothing to say.

Walter notices that Sally has changed her position and is now swimming, breast stroking lazily into deeper water, resting contemplatively and then swimming gracefully in parallel to the shore. Leaving Brian to watch over her, he treks back to his shack, returning with a long towelling bathrobe. It was last worn by his wife, on a night like this, when she too had surrendered to the curative call of the ocean.

Brian is waiting at the waters' edge for Sally as she emerges. He holds the robe out for her to fold herself into. There is no consciousness between them of nudity or modesty, despite having never seen the other naked since they were small children. It doesn't exist in this moment. He supports her gently with just a hand resting under her elbow as they wander back to the shacks. Neither speaks. Sally takes herself to her bedroom, drops the robe to the floor and lowers herself between the sheets. She is asleep in less than a minute.

When Brian returns, Walter is poking the fire and re-stoking it with a couple of mallee roots. He has left Sally's neatly folded clothes on the shack verandah. He lifts the half-full bottle of muscat to Brian in both a salute and an enquiry and sits back in his chair. Brian nods and their glasses are topped up.

"You want to talk? Or, more to the point, do you need to talk?" asks Walter.

"I do. Though it would really help to hear your take on what's just happened. You know women better than I do. Have had an intimate relationship with a woman. I haven't a bloody clue." Brian sips on the muscat. It's too sweet. It no longer fits his mood or the moment.

"Sorry Wal. I can't drink this. I need a drink. I want a whisky. You want one?"

"I was thinking the very same thing myself," laughs Walter. "Yours or mine?"

"Ha. We'll start with mine, knowing we've got yours as a backup." And he strolls into the shack returning with a large bottle of water to reprogram their palates, an unopened bottle of 15-year-old single malt Glenfiddich and two tumblers.

"Hmm. Top shelf I see."

"Well a little higher than the shelf I usually select my whiskies from," smiles Brian. "I was feeling very celebratory in the bottle shop. I still am actually. But this last hour with Sal has shifted it to a whole new level."

"Ah yes. You've mentioned a little of her situation over the years. I'd rather gathered that you had a special loathing for her," Walter pauses to give emphasis, "*Fucking arsehole of a husband,*" successfully parroting Brian's mandatory reference to his brother-in-law. "And seeing you arrive together today, happy and high-spirited, I guessed that she had escaped or run away or is moving out before moving on." He swirls his whisky, holding his glass under his nose, savouring it's peaty aroma before taking a sip.

"Yes. It's been a bloody welcome surprise. Such a relief. Milton and I've been hoping, wishing for this for years. He adores her..... And the boys..... It's really pained him... Well both of us, to see her trapped, stoically putting up with that shithead and just not understanding what has kept her there. Like there's been invisible shackles holding her."

"Has he been physically violent? Bashed or beaten her?"

"She says no. But Milton feels there's been more than him just being a selfish, boorish, ignorant, arrogant, philandering, root rat,..... *a fucking arsehole.*"

Walter chuckles. "Why don't you say what you really think of him?"

Brian laughs, a deep relaxed belly laugh. "Has he been physically violent? Yeah. Well. Who would know? We don't.... and maybe never will." He takes a small mouthful of whisky, holds it in his mouth as it warms his palate, it's heat filtering up through his nostrils. He swallows, feeling its fire flow all the way down to his stomach where it warms and calms and grounds him. No more talk about Andy. It is Sal he needs to focus on, to support. But how? There is too much he doesn't understand, just doesn't know.

Walter gives him time to shift gears, to come back to the intent, the content of their conversation. He's ten years older and feels somewhere between uncle and older brother.

"You know we have been part of a very special moment tonight... It wouldn't have happened if she hadn't felt completely safe." Brian says nothing. "There's been a letting go, an acceptance, a release,... from grief. Not from fear. I don't think Sal has been afraid."

Brian looks directly at him. "How do you know? How can you see this on your first meeting? Do you see it, or feel it, or what?

"I've seen it and sensed it, felt it and lived it... before." He holds his whisky glass in both hands and looks deeply into it. Brian waits.

"Kath showed me,... taught me." He waits. Brian looks at him intently, struggling for words.

"We all miss her Wal. She was special. What you had with her was special." He wants to say, to ask, 'Are you lonely? How much do you miss her? How do you fill the void her dying has left you? Will you ever get over her? Will there ever be anyone else for you?'

Wal continues. "I miss her every day, every moment of every day. I wake and am surprised she's not in the bed beside me. Even momentarily wonder if she's gone for an early morning walk along the beach as she loved to. Or in the kitchen making our coffee... But then she's with me every day... I talk to her.... In my head. I listen to her. I know she is with me, always. I just can't bloody touch her. Kiss the back of her neck. Hold her hand. Have her lean into me. Make love with her." His voice deepens and catches with emotion on the last sentence.

Brian is profoundly moved. "Ah Jesus Wal... I think,... I can imagine how you must feel. Christ I'm so sorry."

Walter rallies. "But then I had all those wonderful years. They weren't always easy mind you. Kath was pretty damaged when we found each other. It took her a long time to trust that I truly loved her, unconditionally. To know what love is... A choice, and what we do, as much if not more than a feeling... And then when she got it, embraced it and applied it to herself, the kids, and to us, the two of us. She shone a whole new light on us all and our world."

"Thank you Wal. We've never talked like this. You're helping me to see a Sal I've not seen before, or... or maybe even she's never been before."

"I told you. We've been witness to something very special tonight. It's precious. Let it be... Just let it be."

Love, understanding, wonder and gratitude well up in Brian from his gut to his heart, a great lump swelling in his throat, tears welling in his eyes. He is filled with a new knowing but has no words.

"I hear you," says Walter softly. "And now my friend it's time for each of us to go to bed."

# Chapter 8

Monday morning

He has slept, but not well. Milton sips on his mug of espresso coffee, relaxing in his favourite place; an old, cracked leather armchair on their deck, a grape vine covered timber indulgence connecting the back verandah to Brian's expansive vegetable garden. It is where they relax, where Brian retreats to smoke, the homophobic free haven for drinkies with yachting mates on summer evenings, and where they hold their more formal dinner parties and extravaganzas. Where Brian indulges his culinary creativity. Where Milton delights in setting the stage for their social intercourse with treasured friends. The large old oak table adorned in crisp white linens, sparkling glasses and dinnerware; fairy lights woven through the grape vines, assorted candles lighting the table and favourite corners of the garden. At one end is a grand stone fireplace that warms them on wintery evenings and which doubles as a BBQ and pizza oven. At the other is a fecund fernery in which are nestled a salacious selection of erotic male sculptures, illuminated by strategically positioned solar spotlights.

Confident Sally and the boys are safe and that he and Brian can provide the support she needs without manipulating her choices, Milton is still restless. He wants to have established strategies, a contingency plan to manage Andy should he need to. He wants to be prepared for the inherently obnoxious behaviours that are likely to follow. Andy's drunken and threatening phone messages have unsettled him. He now knows there is a feral unpredictability about the man, a wild uncensored insanity. Outside his reluctant attendance at infrequent family gatherings, he has had nothing to do with *the Arsehole*. He knows him only through Brian's reminiscences, observations and increasing frustrations.

Brian and Andy are the same age. Andy's parents had been third-generation farmers. Brian's Mum and Dad moved from the city to their rural township to take over a small local transport business which eventually lost its relevance as rail freight was taken over by trucks and semi-trailers. The two families had been acquaintances attending the same community events and celebrations but never socialising together.

Andy, a difficult only child, had been bullied by his father and compensatorily indulged by his mother. He had shared the same year through school as Brian, and despite his oft times chaotic and challenging behaviours, they had been mates. Brian had been a steadying influence, a social anchor; able to disarm Andy's tantrums, disassociating from them as necessary. Andy brought spontaneity and an adventurous energy to their friendship, Brian mostly bemused by his antics and grandiose ideas.

Both left school at sixteen, Andy to work on the farm, Brian to begin his chef's apprenticeship. It was in the following year that they had their tumultuous falling out. Brian was discovering new, different friendships within the hospitality community. He had confessed to his friend that he was attracted more to men than he was to girls. Andy, utterly outraged, had told him he would have nothing to do with a *fucking poofta*. He had then maliciously and hubristically put it around town what had become of their friendship and why.

Brian's Dad very quickly learned of this through the shameless gossip mongers at the local pub. He could have refuted the claims and turned on his son, but chose to confide in Stanley, his friend, to try to best understand homosexuality, if his son may indeed be gay, and how best to support him.

Brian has always spoken with reverence and love of the conversations he had with his Dad and Stanley, learning to know, accept, and trust himself. How to navigate the endemic homophobic seas in his community, choosing where and how to live his life safely, confidently and proudly. His Dad and Stanley had arranged for his apprenticeship to be relocated, facilitating his move to the city, where he was supported by a network of Stanley's friends.

His Mum, as always, stood by him, quietly acknowledging, accepting, what she had always suspected, keeping her thoughts and fears to herself. Sally, five years younger, had been aware of the seriousness of the broken friendship and Brian's leaving, but too young to understand the complexities of the homophobic and hypocritical attitudes that informed many of the choices and behaviours in their small historically conservative country township.

Milton and Brian, at the beginning of their romantic partnership, knew Sally was considering nursing training, having graduated well from school. She had become closer to Andy's mum, Margaret, a nurse, who had fostered that interest over the previous year, even arranging school holi-day work experiences for her. She would have had contact with Andy because of this, but they were never aware of them dating or spending time together.

Brian seldom returned to his parents' home after leav-ing, but even they had proclaimed their bewilderment at her pregnancy and marriage. He has shared with Milton many times since, his confusion over her commitment to the farm, to caring for Margaret during her final debilitated years, and how she compartmentalised her life with Andy.

Despite the warmth and casual comfort of their relation-ships, the topic of her marriage has always been off-limits. She would redirect conversations or just leave, so that he and Brian learned early to not go there. It has, however, remained a frequent topic of discussion between them, an endless enigma. Contemplatively sipping on his coffee, Milton remembers Sal's response to his query as to Andy's propensity to violence. It was considered, commanding, an intensely affirmative statement.

*"He is capable of insane, irrational violence, given the right provocation."* It is the source of his restlessness. Her steely gaze, looking directly into his eyes as she spoke, haunts him. There is so much unsaid. He revisits the conversation.

*"I am not going back. I can't go back. And I want him to know that."*

*"He's always been difficult, been incredibly selfish. He isn't physically violent with me."*

*"He's become increasingly abusive, especially when he's drunk."*

*"He's got progressively worse these last three years since Margaret died. She managed him."*

He must talk to Brian. But is this the right time? Brother and sister are alone together under totally new circumstances. What is happening for the two of them? He wishes not to intrude. His discussions with Brian haven't included the details of the conversation he had with Sal, but he needs him to know. They need to unravel the mystery buried in her words. A door has been unlocked. She has released the seal on the tomb in which an intrinsic part of herself has been so long buried. They need to make sure they do nothing that will cause her to slam that door shut.

He won't phone. He'll text, despite his growing impatience to talk. He'll stifle his inherent impulsivity, intent on respecting and supporting Brian's wonderfully measured way of managing crises, making considered decisions. It is why he is such a great chef. It is why they are so good together. Brian is his rock. He is Brian's playmate, confidante and mentor in the carefree exploration of social and sensual pleasures. He misses him in this moment, wishes he could relax into a warm embrace, fold Brian's head into his shoulder, feel his strong arms around him, smell the cocktail of shampoo and cigarette smoke in his hair, relax into their pattern of long slow synchronised breathing, as one together.

"Hey Bri.
When you have the right moment we need to talk.
I know Sal is safe with you now.
But I'm worried about the Arsehole.
It's what she said. How she said it.
We need to talk. She mustn't know.
Too much missing you!!"

\*\*\*

Monday afternoon.

It is well after midday when Brian discovers Milton's text. He too needs to talk. He wants to share the amazing transformation in Sally last night. Its magic has not faded. She has been both her old self and new self this morning, drifting between moments of quiet reflection and playfulness. Walter joined them for a mid-morning coffee after their leisurely late breakfast and invited her to go fishing. They have arranged to meet around sunset. Sally, lazing in a faded hammock suspended between two verandah posts, is contentedly reading the paperback she picked from the shack's informal library. Brian helps Walter slide one of the dinghies down onto the beach. They refuel and test the outboard motor together.

"It's good having you here with us Wal. Sal is really comfortable with you, and I know she is safe. She feels safe. Thank you."

"It's my pleasure." He pauses. "She's a strong woman. I think she's made difficult decisions and stuck to them. And now's a time of letting them go. I can relate to that. It's a long process. It takes its own time. And this is just the place to do it. Safe. Silent. No pressures. I fill my bucket each time I visit. And she's helping me too you know."

"I need to talk to Millie," says Brian. "He sent me a text. I might make the most of the time you're taking Sal fishing to do that. I'll meet you down on the beach when I'm finished. It's important she doesn't feel we're colluding behind her back." He laughs. "Even if that's exactly what we *are* doing. She knows we love her, and the boys, and'll do what is best for them. But we can't push her, manipulate her. She can smell that rat before we even realise we're doing it! Yep. She's strong. The strongest woman, the strongest person I've ever known. Now, more than ever. We,... I need to be mindful of that."

"Yeah. Don't worry. Already picked up on it anyway. She's special alright. Reminds me of my Kath... A little... In the unsaid ". He is quiet for a moment, reflecting on his feelings. "And that's a real comfort, not a painful memory. I say, thank you Sal." He places his hand on Brian's shoulder as they walk back over the sandy ridge to the shacks.

* * *

Monday evening

"Well, a great idea but the fish must have got wind of our intentions," laughs Walter as he cradles the mug of coffee that Sally has poured for him from the thermos she brought with them. They have had the odd nibble but no bites. Not a hint of a catch.

"Do you want to go in? Though it's a great night to be out on the ocean."

"I'd like to stay," says Sally. "Actually, there is something I'd like your help with Wal. And I don't want to talk about it in front of Brian." She pauses, choosing her words carefully. "It's a private matter. I need to have it sorted before he learns about it. It's to do with the farm. The title. The finances. I know you'll know what I might need to do or at least who I need to talk to. It's complicated.' She hesitates. This is so hard. It's got to be done. She has been instinctively drawn to Walter and knows she can trust him.

"We have an accountant but no family lawyer. I don't trust myself to find who I need. I don't even know where to start looking. I need someone completely separate, away from where I've been living, new to my life and situation....... Unbiased but knowledgeable."

Walter nods, knowing too well the drawback of living in a small rural community. "Of course. If I can. Farming finances and families are tricky at the best of times. But when there's a split; a spouse leaving, brothers falling out, it can get really ugly. I've seen it before." Sally is slow to respond. She sighs.

"When Andy's Dad died, the farm was left to his mum, Margaret. Not long after, I discovered I was pregnant, and we got married. It was agreed that the farm would be left to Andy and me both, in joint tenancy, so that if either of us died, it would go to the other, and by default to our children thereafter. It was a condition of our marriage, that Margaret's will first be changed to reflect that. I would only agree to the marriage on those terms." She sighs deeply, all the while looking out into the endless shadows of the night sky, unable to look directly at Walter. He sits quietly, attentively, his eyes glued to the base of the boat.

"She had her first stroke when the boys were eight. I insisted she change the title on the farm to them, joint ownership, joint tenancy, held in trust until they are eighteen, with me as the sole trustee. Andy doesn't know this. He has just assumed that we are joint owners.

"I have always been the business manager. I was the executor of Margaret's will. It had lost its relevance when she died anyway. He had no wish to be involved. He's actually not very clever; and knows he's not, so avoids situations where that ignorance might be on display. I have taken advantage of that... And I have no shame in saying so."

This is more complex than Walter has imagined. He realizes the relationship between Sally and Andy is not the issue. She's well on top of it, and probably always has been. It is the relationship that she had with her mother-in-law that seems to have dominated her choices.

"May I ask you a question? And please tell me if I'm intruding." Sally turns her head to look him straight in the eyes. There is trust and truth in her gaze.

"It's okay. You need to know how and why this has become so complicated. You're the only person I know that can help me with this. You've no emotional,... or financial... or historical investment in any of it. Not like Brian and Millie. I know they worry for me. And they both despise Andy.

"Their desire to punish him would cloud their judgements, pervert their advice. And I don't trust a lawyer or professional advisor to understand. There's too much of my past I just don't wish to tell them. My choices, my manipulations... Not that I'm ashamed. I'm not. I just don't know if I can trust them to respect my wishes.... To respect me." She becomes flustered, struggling to find the words to best explain herself.

"I worry they could push me to accept their legal and financial protocols, to change *my* wishes to fit." She is still and silent, thinking. "I don't know how, but I know you see me........you understand... Me!!"

"Was your mother-in-law a dominating woman?" asks Brian gently. "Did she manipulate you? It is a common story on farms and in families where women have subordinate roles and identities. The husband's mother indulging her son, in blatant or covert opposition to her daughter-in-law. Manipulating him, emotionally blackmailing him, pulling the financial and inheritance strings to get what she thinks is right. To get what *she* wants."

"If anything, it was the opposite. I had the power over Margaret. She wanted the marriage when I went to her pregnant with the boys. I made it perfectly clear I would not be relinquishing them for adoption. And she wanted to avoid a scandal at any cost. She was never in doubt that I was pregnant to Andy........ I set the terms. She lived with us in the farmhouse until she died..... Well, it was really more a case of me moving in with them. Ours was not a normal marriage."

She rests with this last statement, considering where to go with her explanation. How much of her story needs to be told? How much of that painful past is she prepared to revisit? Is this the time to set it free? Is she ready?

"I was young. I was just eighteen, but I refused to be treated as a child. She was a nurse and worked in community health up until her stroke. We negotiated and agreed on separate domestic and business domains. I called the shots. I don't know where I got the balls to do it really. I just knew instinctively that I needed to take control,..... from the beginning. I was having twins. I had no means of being independent. I was not going to impose my predicament on Mum and Dad or Brian. I was determined that Margaret and Andy both be forced to face *their* responsibilities. I was not going to carry it all on my own.

"Andy is a competent farmer and has always made the practical decisions in that regard, conferring with me, depending on me, to manage the finances, the business. The business too, has been in our joint names since we married. But he was the passenger, dependent on each of us in very different ways... Ours was not a normal marriage."

She finds herself wringing her hands and stops, wiping them backwards and forwards on her jeans, before leaning over to trail first one and then the other in the water. It calms her. She is silent, Walter resting, waiting respectfully beside her. She raises her hands to hold a palm on each cheek, resting her cool fingers gently against closed eyelids. She breathes in deeply, sighs once, then inhales the oceanic air again. The stillness anchors her and a calm clarity returns.

"Andy was his mother's life, her reason for being. She pampered him,... mollycoddled him; so that he never really grew up. He had no reason to, no need to. And likewise, the twins have been my only focus, since before they were born, from the first moment I felt them move inside me... They have been my purpose, my responsibility to.... to...." She seems lost for a moment in her recollections, considering them, deciding what she will say next.

"Margaret loved them. Yes she loved them... in a detached sort of way. They were of her son. But it was always about Andy! Theirs really was an emotionally incestuous relationship. Yet the irony is, he's spent most of his adult life rebelling. Drinking, fighting, philandering."

She snorts a mocking laugh. "He's branded locally as *the town root rat*. I don't know how he does it. There must be some truly frustrated, desperate or just plain stupid women out there. At the same time he was hopelessly dependent on his mother, and then me... It's only since she died that I've come to really know this. Since the boys have gone away to school and I've had time, made time, to process it. To understand his animosity, his belligerence. How I've enabled it... Never called him on it.

"Stanley has helped enormously. He was Dad's friend. He's gay. He's our local Anglican minister. He's been my confidante over the years, my spiritual mentor if you like, but he can't help me with this." She smiles a weary smile. "I knew I couldn't trust her.... Margaret. She had betrayed me before. It would always be about Andy with her, never be about me or the twins... Always Andy. Her Andy." She is immersed in this, remembering, and trails a hand in the waters again. Walter waits for her to continue.

"I needed to ensure my boys' futures. I learned early... to anticipate her cunning, to manipulate her,... and Andy... To manipulate them both. Planting seeds, feeding them, so that farming and business ideas appeared to be theirs." She is now running her hands up and down along her thighs, anxiety threatening to overwhelm her; this explanation feeling more like a confession. It *is* a confession.

"We both knew, Margaret and I, that she would become physically and financially dependent on me, not Andy. He's a child. She had nowhere to go. All her earnings had been invested in the farm. I managed the finances. Controlled them. I had the skills. She didn't. Her husband had held the purse strings. She, like each of us, had a personal allowance, but that's all it was, spending money, to accommodate our immediate personal needs, our individual choices. Not enough to do anything with."

She looks straight at Walter and offers him a weak smile, pausing almost for dramatic effect. "I blackmailed her."

Stunned by such a candid confession, Walter asks, "How so?"

"I promised to care for her for as long as she needed, on condition she transfer the farm titles to the boys while she was still able, and seen to be able. We both knew there would likely be another stroke before long. And there was. The week after the papers were signed."

"And if she refused?"

"She would go into a nursing home. She was a nurse. She knew what that would be like. It was her greatest fear. Andy doesn't know. I didn't need to make that a condition. She couldn't bring herself to tell him anyway. Beneath her maternal manipulations she too was a coward."

"Did you hate her? Fear her? Disdain her?"

"No. In many ways, I still cared about her. She had had a difficult marriage with Andy's father. Her work had been her escape and identity. We had always been friends. A bit like sisters, there for each other. Riding the ebb and flow of power in our relationship, depending on changing situations, conflicting choices." Her voice falters. She is again back in that time, revisiting a place she has long moved on from. Tears are suddenly welling in her eyes.

"She did let me down big time... Once. I understood why.... I forgave her. But everything... everything changed after that when I discovered I was pregnant with the twins." She raises a hand to wipe a tear rolling forlornly down one cheek.

"I'm taking us in now," says Walter. "It's time to be on solid ground."

* * *

They have pulled the dinghy high up onto the beach and are sitting several metres away, both instinctively removing sandals, stretching their toes rhythmically in the warm sand, stilling their fidget feelings. Sally smoothes herself a potential slate with wide sweeps of her right hand, pausing every few strokes to trickle sand through open fingers. Walter rolls himself a cigarette and draws on it deeply, that first inhalation slowing his racing thoughts, tempering his rising emotions. He is surprised by his growing compassion for this woman; her deep woundedness rising from the depths of her soul like a corpse, to float gently between them.

"Sal, I can help you. I know just the right person. She's a very experienced Family Law lawyer. My niece. And I will walk beside you, for as long as you need. It will be my privilege." She is silent, not yet ready to respond, considering where to go with this conversation.

Walter has enough information for now, but she wants to tell him more. She needs to set it free. She is afraid that this opportunity may not surface again. The ocean, the cover of night, this place, this time, this man, combining to gift her the opportunity to release her burden; the secret she has carried for so long. Too long. She is weary and wants to be free.

He senses her indecisiveness. "We don't have to do this now. I can see how stressful it is for you."

"No.... I have to... I want to.... To get it out.

"I've never told anyone. Only Stanley knows. He was there for me back then... has always been. It has been our secret. He respects, protects my silence, my choices." Her voice has lowered, slowed, coming from deep within.

"It's time... Time to speak my truth... Time to set it free... Will you be my witness?" She reaches out to hold his hand and looks into his eyes, searching, finding the courage she knew would be reflected in them. She releases him to look once again out across the ocean. Neither are aware that Brian has paused at the ridge of sand behind them. He stops, unable, and not trying, to clearly hear their voices. He hesitates, just briefly, then turns away, leaving. This moment belongs to them.

"Ours was not a normal marriage." Strange that she continues to think of it, speak of it, in the past. It is but days since she failed to step off that bus. It seems so long ago, so enormous is the shift.

"I was pregnant, nearly five months pregnant when we married. I didn't truly believe it until I was maybe twelve weeks. I had suspected it. Feared it. I couldn't.... I wouldn't believe it. And I waited another four weeks before I confronted Margaret. I wanted her to take responsibility. For what had happened, with Andy.

" She knew... She chose him over me... To protect him... As always. Excusing his behaviours, his cowardice, not making him take responsibility." Sally realises she is rambling. Walter is listening intently.

"It happened when his dad died. He had a brain cancer. It didn't take long after his diagnosis. Maybe six weeks. He insisted Margaret look after him at home, which she did. And I helped. Even staying in the house with them the last two weeks.

"He'd always been such a bombastic bully with Andy, but mellowed in the final days, when he knew he had so little time left. They had a reconciliation of sorts. Andy and Margaret were with him when he died.

"It happened sooner, more quickly than I expected. I had gone to bed. I got up when I heard Andy's muffled sobbing.

He was bereft. Margaret stayed with her husband. I was in my pyjamas, comforting Andy. Holding him. Made him a cup of tea and encouraged him outside, to sit with me on the verandah. I remember it was a very still night; and moonlight.

"Andy calmed down but then switched to his argumentative, belligerent self. He's unable to be present with softer emotions. He can only see the world through his own warped narcissistic window. His comfort place is in criticising, shaming or bullying others, as his father always had with him.

"He started bagging me about my plans to go to nursing school, to be a nurse. Then he turned on Brian. Pushing the *fucking poofta* platform he inflicts on anybody and everybody." She pauses, considers what she will say next. Talking more to herself than to Walter.

"It was my fault in a way. I goaded him. I was so sick of him, his selfishness.... I was tired. He was so ungrateful, so critical of everyone. And when he started bagging Brian... Brian who never hurt anyone.... I just flipped. I told him he was a hypocrite. Reminded him how they had been friends for so many years. Told him that at least Brian was honest about who he is, his sexuality, and doesn't pretend to be other than his true self.

"I told him he was full of shit, a root rat, pretending to be the big macho man when he was probably denying that he had really wanted Brian for himself. That he resented him being attracted to other men and taking himself away." She releases an enormous sigh.

"I don't know where it all came from. Probably my idle thoughts about him over the years just spewing out all at once. If I hadn't..... It wouldn't have happened." Head down, she is talking into the sand; struggling, with memories and emotions threatening to overwhelm her. She knows what she wants to say, just not how to say it.

"He... he was furious... Just switched completely... Switched to this steely silent rage. Not a word.... His eyes on fire... He grabbed my hair... so violently... wrenching my head back. I could barely breath... And then he raped me."

This last statement sits heavily between them. Walter has no words. He waits in silence for Sally to continue, when she is ready, if she is able.

"And Margaret *saw* it. She knew.... She *knew*. She did *nothing*... And she knew, I knew, she'd seen it... I was so shocked. I couldn't speak. I could barely breathe. In that moment I believed it was my fault. I believed that she would blame me." She rests in silence. Walter knows she has more to say. He waits. It is not yet time for him to speak.

"Andy stormed off to the shed. I went to my bedroom, dressed, and drove to Stanley's house behind the church."

She is now weeping, tears rolling freely down her cheeks. Walter, eyes down, gazing blindly at the sand, knows this by the change in her breathing. She inhales sharply with a shudder.

"I was *so ashamed*. I really believed it was *my fault*."

"It is *never* the woman's fault. It was *not* your fault," says Walter tenderly.

"That's what Stanley said... He was so understanding.... Held me close, saying nothing, just holding me until I stopped shaking." She releases another involuntary shuddering sigh.

"He asked me what I wanted, not once telling me what I should do. Offering to take me to hospital or to the Police station but totally accepting my choice not to. He's such a beautiful man." She resumes her weeping. He wants to hold her close, to comfort her, as he comforted his Kath in their early years, once she trusted him enough to show him her broken self.

Sally shudders again. "I was *so ashamed*. And then.... *pregnant.*"

Walter waits, his heart open, breaking with hers in empathy. The ache of compassion expands in his chest; he is so deeply moved by her story, knows she is revisiting it, telling it, for the first time. He knows too that she can tell it to him, who knows pain and loss, and powerlessness. Brian is too close, translating her choices of the last eighteen years, as seen through his own biased window, creating his own story of her. She has so long held onto this story; her story, her secret life.

They sit in companionable silence for a time. Walter rolling and smoking another cigarette. Sally, now completely calm, is again smoothing the sand in wide sweeps, trickling it through open fingers, deep in thought. There seems nothing more to be said but neither is ready to leave.

Eventually she asks, "Wal, have you been with anyone since your wife died?"

"No." He is surprised but not offended.

"Have you ever been with anyone else?"

"No. Kath was my first and only. She was experienced and brought that to our marriage."

"Were you good together?" He hesitates, unsure where this conversation is going. There is both a naivete and a worldliness in her questions and demeanour. He looks to her, but she keeps her eyes lowered, focussing on the rhythmic swirling patterns she is making in the sand.

"We were, but not always. Kath was a very sexual woman and that was exciting, to begin with, but it took her a long time to learn to be intimate, emotionally intimate, sensually intimate. She had to learn to trust; to trust herself more than me. And then........ it was good. Beautiful.... Till the end."

"I've never been with anyone." Sally stills her hands and looks up at Walter. "I have sometimes wondered what it might be like." She hesitates. "Ours was *not* a *normal* marriage. There was no sex. No physical contact. We had separate beds, separate bedrooms. From the moment I moved in."

Walter doesn't know what to say. Where is she going with this?

"I would like to have sex one day. To make love with someone I trust. No, have them make love to me. I don't know how."

"It just happens, with the right person, at the right time." Walter smiles. "And in the right place."

Sally too smiles. He is so kind, so gentle, so generous in sharing his truth. No wonder she has been so comfortable in sharing her own truth with him.

"I trust you." She says. "I would like you to show me... One day... Not now. When I'm ready.... I'm not ready yet."

He stands. "Will you walk with me Sal? And hold my hand."

They leave their sandals nestled in the sand, marking the narrow track through the dunes back to the shacks. Their hands are warm and dry. The comfortable, genderless, benign grip of friends, the mutual meeting of ageless souls. The night is neither warm nor chilled; that too benign, and perfectly still. They can see lights blinking and flashing out to sea; dinghies and their occupants drifting between cray-pots, trolling for tailor.

# Chapter 9

Tuesday morning

Brian is pouring his second cup of coffee before he suspects Sally is not in her room. He knocks gently and peeps in. Her bed has been slept in but is empty. Has she returned to be with Walter after he dropped her off at their shack last night? She had been in a very quiet, introspective mood, not at all her relaxed playful self. She had wished him goodnight and gone immediately to bed. He'd stayed out on the shack verandah, smoking, mulling over his conversation with Millie.

All is not as he, they, have believed it to be. Sally's marriage to Andy, her resolute determination to remain on the farm, to care for Margaret all those years. It remains a mystery, now even more so. With this sudden change though, too many of the long-held parameters are shifting. But in what direction? It's as though the layers of neatly stacked boxes that have held her life are sliding apart, gradually collapsing, and all they can do is just hold on and wait to see where they slide to. He wanders out onto the shack verandah, contemplatively sipping his coffee. Walter is walking towards him, rod and tackle box in hand, obviously intending to do some beach fishing.

Brian asks, "Is Sal with you?"

"No... I've not seen her since I dropped her off last night. She alright?"

"I'm not sure. I'm not worried, but I think we should check." He leaves his coffee mug on the verandah edge as they head over the sandhill ridge towards the beach. Sally, stick in hand, is drawing on the wet sand. She has already placed a collection of seaweed, smooth pebbles and drift-wood in an expansive circular pattern. Barefoot, in a loose, waisted dress, tangled hair blowing free, she is immersed in this carefree creative quest. She reminds him of the image he once had of the short story character, Cassie, a Scottish water sprite who volunteers for an anti-fracking protest. He grins affectionately.

"Let me get you a coffee," he says to Walter as they retreat back to the shacks.

"I'd prefer tea, actually. Strong white with two sugars. Long-time farming habit," replies Walter as he rests his fishing gear on the verandah and pulls up a chair.

"Millie and I are worried about Andy." Brian hands him his mug of tea. "Well, not worried so much, just precaution-arily concerned. More about Sal's material security than her physical safety. We believe we have that covered. But he's such a bloody loose cannon."

"Don't worry. Sal's on top of it. She's asked for my help; being a farmer and having a working knowledge of farming business." He blows across his mug and takes a cautious sip. "There are some complications. I'm getting onto my niece, she's a lawyer. Yeah, Jennifer will be able to sort it. I guess Sal will fill you in when she's ready."

He chuckles. "She's a very independent, strong-minded woman, that sister of yours." He looks at his watch. "So what's the time now? We agreed to have a telephone meeting later this morning. And Sal wants to buy a new mobile phone. But it's not urgent while she has access to ours."

"When is young Joey returning to pick you up? asks Brian "I've been wondering if you might be able to stay here a bit longer. Just be here for her. She's taken a real shine to you Wal. She trusts you. Just until we get her sorted."

"No worries." replies Walter as he takes a long swig of his tea. "Joey's back home tomorrow. I've already told him I'm staying on a bit. And I'm only too happy to help. Sal is good for me too, you know. I've been pretty lonely since Kath." He laughs, "Actually, I've already agreed with her to stay longer. So we're all on the same page then."

"And so we are!" Sally is shaking herself free of beach sand. She had heard the last of their conversation. "I didn't sneak up on you" she laughs. "You just didn't hear me coming. I'll have my shower and be dressed in a jiffy. I'm starving. What's for breakfast?"

\* \* \*

She is adamant she does not want Brian present during her phone call with Jennifer. She and Walter use his mobile on speaker on his shack verandah where there is good reception and she can sit at the outdoor setting to comfortably make notes. She has, in preparation, made a list of dot points of statements and questions. Brian meanwhile has driven to town to top up fridge and pantry stocks and buy her a new mobile phone.

"Are you happy with where we got to today?" asks Walter, once the phone call is over. "Jennifer seems really confident."

"More than happy. I was imagining it would be much more difficult. With the farm title already in the boys names, my sole trustee status in place, gaining sole interim custody is not at all complicated. Though that actually hasn't been my concern. Andy has never had any interest in the boys. Extricating myself from the farm business has been my biggest worry."

"Well, that too is only as complicated as you allow it to be. As you found out. It's when we doggedly hold onto financial and material expectations, not prepared to accept anything less than what we believe we are owed, that the potentially ugly and ego-driven tug-o-wars begin. I'm really proud of you Sal. After all the time and work and effort you've obviously invested in that business, to just walk away."

"I know Jennifer's advice stressed my entitlement to half share of the working capital and business assets; and yes, that money would help my transition to a new life, to get resettled. But I only want the monies owed to me. Nothing else. I read a quote once which said, 'No price we pay for freedom is ever greater than the cost of living without it.' It has always stayed with me. I wrote it on a card and kept it in my wallet. In fact, I think it may still be there." She laughs.

"Look, the boys educational and financial futures are secure until they're ready to make their own life choices. That was always my priority. I've become multi-skilled over the years and I'm confident I can earn a wage, start a business, pay my way. With Brian and Millie ever my supporters, I'll always have somewhere to land. I just don't want any of the emotional or historical baggage that comes with anything belonging to that farm, that house, that partnership.' She grins at him over the top of her coffee mug and exclaims satirically, "I just want to be free!"

"Jennifer said she'd have the affidavits and other documents ready for me to sign tomorrow afternoon. I'm sure Brian'll be happy to take us. I'm thinking we'll need to stay over." She looks eagerly towards him. "You will come with me, won't you? I'm sure Jennifer would want to see you."

"Sal," he says smiling, "I said I would walk alongside you through this for as long as you need me to. It won't be for long. You'll see."

\* \* \*

Wednesday evening

"Oooh. I sensed a celebration in the air." Milton bursts onto the deck where Brian, Sally and Walter have been sitting drinking coffee. He thrusts two bottles of his favourite Chardonnay Pinot Noir at Brian. "Pop one of these darl, while I go get the glasses and some ice."

"So have you been waiting long?" He returns with four wine flutes, a bucket of ice, and a crisp white linen napkin draped over his arm.

"No. About half an hour. Millie, Walter may prefer a Scotch or a beer to wine," he replies, turning in his chair to take the bucket. The ice rattles as he inserts one bottle before expertly popping the cork on the other.

"Maybe later. I'm happy with this celebratory choice. It has been a good day, I think," says Walter, smiling at Sally who grins back. She is glowing.

Brian stands to pour the wine; Milton returns with serviettes and an antipasto platter, the latter obviously lifted from the restaurant kitchen at his work. He is ever the master of organisation, making perfect catering comforts magically appear. He takes his glass from Brian and resting a hand affectionately on Sally's shoulder, thrusts it high as he exclaims;

"To Sal, coming home at last. To Walter, our shining knight, arriving just when we need you." He looks at Brian with great affection, "To us!"

Walter too stands and the three men raise their glasses, clinking them with each other, and in turn with Sally, before they drink. She stands, placing her glass on the table and hugs each of them, first Milton, then Brian and finally Walter, murmuring into each of their chests, "Thank you." She and Walter are hugging for the first time. They linger in this new embrace. He rests his lips into her hair and murmurs back, "You're welcome." Brian and Milton look to each other and smile, happily immersing themselves in this magnetic moment.

Walter and Brian have switched to Scotch and soda. Milton and Sally, on their second glass of wine, have had to dip into the second bottle. Conversation has been a cross between trivial and whimsical. Kelsie returned Sal's car and left a gift package of her Nonna's Italian baking on the seat with a message that Milton's car will be ready for pick up on Saturday. Milton has arranged rostered time off until and including then. How might they make best use of that time? Talking about anything and everything except what Brian and Milton most want to hear.

Their unspoken curiosity the elephant in the room, Sally initiates the directional change in conversation.

"I met Jennifer, Wal's niece this afternoon. She is lovely." She looks at Walter and smiles. "Wal stayed with me while we confirmed my intentions and I signed all the papers. Wal, you are becoming my very best friend," she laughs and looks to Brian, "After Stanley, that is."

"Jennifer advised from the start that a speedy assertive action is the best option. The affidavits and other papers will be served on Andy tomorrow. I've decided not to stay, not to be anywhere near during that process.' She looks at Millie. 'But we'll definitely need beds here tonight."

"Perfect!" he exclaims.

"And Millie, I'd like you to return with us to the shacks tomorrow. I would like us all safe together until this business is over."

"Done. I'm due for some salty sunshine and sand between my toes."

Sally's tone shifts a gear, becoming more measured and serious. "But first there is something else I have to tell you. There is much you both don't know. I've been keeping... I've been living a secret... Well, a couple of secrets, all these years. Not because I wanted to, but because I had to... Stanley knows all of it... Andy knows some of it. He has been at the centre of it... well... except for the boys.... They have been the reason for it... for it all."

Stemming the urge to speak, Brian looks meaningfully at Milton, willing that he too curb his curiosity. All three men are sitting respectfully and empathetically in wait for her to say what she wants in her own time. She sips on her wine.

"First up. The farm business is in joint names, so that includes the business banking account, the machinery, all the assets, the insurances. A. L. Chester and Co. I am the Co. It has been that way.... It was put in place when we married. At that time also, Margaret's will was changed to pass the farm to Andy and me in joint tenancy. That is what Andy believes has happened." Another sip of wine. "He doesn't know that when Margaret had her first stroke, I insisted that she change the farm title to be in the boys' names, in partnership, joint tenancy; with me as sole trustee until they turn eighteen. That is the second secret.

"So he will be thinking, backed up by the bush lawyers at the pub," she raises her eyebrows and releases a heavy sigh, "that he owns half the farm, half the assets and half the money in the bank, apart from what sits in our individual personal accounts.

"He has no idea how to manage money, how any of the finances work. I have always kept the books, since we were married. I learned from Mum, with her and Dad's business. Margaret too, didn't have a clue. Andy's Dad had always done it all. She really didn't have any choice.

"I am the sole trustee for the boys' educational trust account. And Brian you have been my nominated proxy should anything happen to me." She drains her wine glass and holds it out to Milton for a refill, in need of the activity of drinking, not the alcohol. Although it is certainly helping to mitigate her dread and discomfort.

"From the very beginning my choices have been for the boys. I wanted them to have strong foundations, knowing who they are, where they come from, that they are loved, that they matter. Not the illegitimate offspring of the girl just out of school who couldn't keep her legs together."

She sighs and looks into her wineglass. "Stanley helped me to work out what *I* wanted for myself, and for my babies. I want you to know these choices have been *mine.*"

"I was determined to be their mother and *care* for them, and *raise* them, and not hand them over to babysitters, child carers or family. Anyone else who would impose *their* child rearing values, *their* priorities and *their* agendas on my boys. All the while having to work in whatever unskilled job I could find to support us all. And I didn't want to be accepting handouts, bailouts, from you and Mum and Dad. I knew that if I was dependent on the support of family, I would feel obliged to listen, to consider everyone's opinions." She pauses to take a swallow of wine and turns to speak directly to Brian.

"You know what Mum and Dad were like. They were fantastic parents. But I would always be their child and treated accordingly. I had to be the adult, not the child. I had to be... I wanted to be adult and seen as such. Not beholden to my parents, having to qualify every choice, qualify every decision I made, on a daily basis.

"They were as shocked as you when I was pregnant, got married and moved out. But by getting married and moving in with Margaret and Andy, without discussing it with any of you or anyone beforehand; you all had to just accept it. What could you do?

"I was determined Matt and Benjie were going to have a proper education and the best opportunity for their futures. The farm is theirs. Andy can't change that. He will be seriously pissed off when he finds out."

Brian, unable to contain himself any longer asks. "And the first secret?" Sally steels herself, looks to Walter and feels the courage he is willing her.

"Ours was not a normal marriage. It was a business arrangement. Right from the beginning." She sips on her wine. "I went to Margaret when I knew I was pregnant, well when I couldn't deny the fact to myself any longer... to get her, and by default Andy, to take responsibility. I told her straight up I would *not* be getting an abortion. It was too late anyway. And I would *not* be giving them up for adoption. I told her Andy was the father but she already knew that.... And she knew, I knew, she knew.

"Andy was present at that initial confrontation but said nothing... did nothing... letting his mother do all the talking. It was, in effect, between Margaret and me. And always has been." She sighs wearily, takes another sip of her wine. "Andy is a bully, so was his father, but underneath he's a coward. A pathetic, spineless, ignorant coward." She slowly twirls her wine glass in her hands, looking into it for the rest of her explanation.

"Margaret didn't want a scandal. I didn't want my boys growing up as a target for malicious gossip and teasing. You know what the town is like. Their incestuous curiosity feeding on peoples' misfortunes, spreading gossip and misinformation. Making assumptions which are then carried as fact. It was Margaret who first suggested the marriage. We discussed how it might work, but *I* set the conditions. Andy essentially had no say in it. He was the maker of the mayhem, but had nowhere to go."

Sally knows she is going to have to tell them how she got pregnant. She can't give the explanation she gave to Wal. She wishes to spare Brian, and Milton. She wishes to spare herself. She takes a long swallow of wine and considers her words carefully. It is important she reaffirm the choices she made with regard to her marriage, and her reasons.

"The marriage was purely a business arrangement. One that benefited me, and protected the boys. I would have equity in the farm business and financial control over my future. Financial security and stability for my boys." Another sip of wine and she continues.

"I never had a sexual relationship with Andy." There! It has been said.

"The boys were conceived the night Andy's father died. I had been helping Margaret, helping them all out. Those last few weeks before he died. " She says with clear finality. "It was non-consensual sex. I am not telling you how. Not now. It was the one and only time."

Brian and Milton both are shocked. They both gasp in unison.

"Oh Sal." Brian speaks first. "All these years.... Half your life... You were just eighteen! My God... How have you..." He is unable to finish. Milton, uncharacteristically, is mute, completely gobsmacked.

"I went to Stanley when it happened. He helped me then... and when I realised I was pregnant. He has been there for me ever since. Just as he counselled you to know and live your truth;" she says to Brian, "he helped me to find and live mine." She drains her wine glass and holds it forth yet again. Waiting for the refill before continuing.

"And that is all I wish to say on that. It has almost been harder saying it, admitting it, than it has been living it. I will explain.... Another time." She inhales and exhales deeply. Once, twice, three times, consciously following her breath each time. "And now it is over... At last... It is truly over... I can hardly believe it."

And now her truth is where she has needed it to be. Keeping this secret from Brian and Millie, for so long, has been such a burden. While protecting them, or protecting herself, she doesn't know; other than that in maintaining the secret, she has never had to qualify or explain her choices. She has never had them offering or promoting alternatives. She turns to gaze up into the sky. Searching? For what? Messaging? To whom? She looks back at her brother and his adorable, adoring lover, and with absolute finality asks, "Now you two, what's for dinner?"

* * *

Milton returns with a tray of coffee after he and Brian have cleared the dishes. Sally has returned to sobriety, her uncharacteristic sculling of wine discontinued. She has been drinking water and now looks forward to a Millie special coffee, and the after dinner Millie special chocolates. She is feeling much loved and supported by these three men who have made her their priority today, tonight and tomorrow.

This too is a uniquely new experience, apart from Stanley who seems always to have been there. But with him it has been different. While they have an exclusive relationship, friendship, she is in no doubt that he provides comparable emotional, spiritual and psychological support to others, his very special wisdom without judgement or preaching. He seems to have always lived his life purpose, his mission, being of service not just to his church and congregation, but to his community and the people in it, regardless of their religious beliefs or affiliations.

"Brian, Millie, sit down. Now I want to tell you what is in the papers being served on Andy tomorrow. Wal already knows. I want you both to know as well. You have been *so* patient for *so* long. I know I haven't been easy." She rests her mug of coffee on the table, then picks it up again, recognising unconsciously that she can only say what needs to be said if she has something to anchor her hands. She has everyone's attention. Brian and Milton have been impatiently but respectfully waiting for this moment.

"There will be the legal letter informing him of the boys ownership of the farm, explaining when that was implemented and a copy of the title. There will be the notification of the interim custody affidavit that will go to the Magistrate's Court on Friday. This will stay in place for three months by which time I'll be seeking sole custody and guardianship. It will include instructions on what his options are and advising he seek legal advice and representation."

Now for the financial arrangements. She knows Brian and Millie will disapprove. They have no idea how ignorant and incompetent Andy is of business and financial matters. And she doesn't want to punish him. He's been totally dependent on her. She has acknowledged her role in making him so. For the term of their marriage she has seeded and sustained his powerlessness. That, has been his punishment. It is over. Finished. She needs to leave with structures in place to support his transition. It will be up to him how he manages that. Only then can *she* truly be free.

"Depending on seasonal income, Andy and I have each been paid personal allowances. Right from the start, I insisted on my own separate money, a token wage for the domestic and farm work I was doing. In the beginning Margaret's salary ensured that was possible. Andy has had to manage his own personal and social spending. I refused to have anything to do with it. If he needed or wanted extra, I got the same. So I have transferred those funds for the next quarter. I've done the same for the business lease of the farm into the boys' trust account. Andy doesn't know about that either. He won't be happy. The lease contract expires when they turn eighteen. It will need to be renegotiated then.

"I am giving formal notice of leaving the partnership immediately, so that I'm not liable for any debts or expenses. I'm also relinquishing any claim to existing funds, assets or pending income." She hears an involuntary intake of breath from Millie. Brian disguises his dismay by reaching for another cigarette. He and Millie lock eyes. They are both rendered speechless in joint disbelief, disappointment and displeasure. Sally is not surprised at their barely disguised responses.

"I have arranged for our accountant to be financial Power of Attorney. Andy of course will have to agree. But he knows he's completely incapable of managing the finances, or making any financial decisions. So all this will be laid out in very simple terms for him tomorrow. The Process Server will only be able to advise him where he can go to get help understanding what has been served on him. They'll not be answering any other questions. I hope whoever it is, is experienced. Actually, I suggested that they take a support person or Police escort."

Brian can't contain himself any longer. "Sal you're just walking away and leaving him everything. After all these years, your commitment, your hard work. What about you?"

"I'm leaving with my integrity intact; with *no* strings, *no* encumbrances. There will be no room for Andy, his lawyer, or *anyone*, to challenge or criticise my decisions. I have left him, but not totally abandoned him. I am doing this for *me*, not him. I don't want *any*,......not *any* responsibilities; real or emotional. I want to be free. *Totally* free. It is costing me nothing in real terms." She smiles and raises both hands. "Do you see?"

"I'm trying," says Millie. "We both just want more for you."

"What I'm giving myself is my freedom. Immediate. Absolute. Don't underestimate the power in that. I haven't just walked away. I have very consciously set myself free. Stanley and I've had many conversations about freedom over the years. What it means. What entraps us. What holds us back. Money, material possessions, emotional and historical expectations, real or imagined responsibilities. The anchors preventing us from flying. That's what has kept me locked in that place all these years. It's over. It.. is.. finished!" She has been holding her coffee mug in both hands, twisting and turning it as she speaks. She places it firmly on the table and says with a grin. "I'm ready to fly."

# Chapter 10

Friday morning

Jim Kessel is pulling a purple and lime green knitted tea cosy onto their old brown china teapot when he hears the first gunshot. He hesitates as the toaster enthusiastically pops four crispy brown slices, almost ejecting them out onto the Laminex bench top. He hears another two gunshots as he is spreading a generous curve of butter onto each slice; two for himself with vegemite and two for Janice with marmalade. She is tying the sash of her old burgundy dressing gown as she waddles into the kitchen, her matching down at heel slippers shuffling along the well-worn linoleum floor.

"Is that gunshots? she asks, running her knobbled fingers through her dishevelled hair and peering out the window. "Sounds like it's coming from Andy's." There are another three shots and dogs barking frantically as Jim takes himself to the back gate. From there he can pass through the feral hedge to look across the paddock dividing their properties. After a minute or two there is another shot and the immediate screaming of a dog in pain. A second shot and the dog wail ceases. This is repeated with a second dog.

"Jesus. The mad bastard's just killed his dogs." yells Jim. There is another volley of gunshots, a pause which suggests the gun is being reloaded, followed by a series of well-spaced shots.

"What's he shooting at now? Where are the cattle? Not in the house paddock are they? Aah Jesus bloody Christ. I reckon he's shooting Sal's chooks." The gunshots have ceased and Jim hears the front-end loader start up. Andy is obviously drunk, or in a hysterical mood, but most likely both. The roar of the loader's engine revving robustly, reverberates along the valley. He returns to the house, Janet with her toast in hand, waiting expectantly for him on the verandah.

"I'm driving over. Phone Rachel. Tell her what's goin' on and that we'll probably need her. Tell her to get her brothers here. I've gotta a feelin'; yep, I've gotta real bad feelin' about this. It's gonna be a big day." He hitches his trousers up, flipping his braces over each shoulder, takes his keys from their hook near the back door and begins ambling across to where his ute is parked.

He stops, turns, and yells back towards Janice, "It d be a good idea if them fellas bring a bushfire tank and pump. Ya never know what this mad bastard could get up to." He turns and continues mumbling all the way to the shed. "Yep. It's gonna be a big day. I can feel it. Ya just know when things are gonna turn. The stupid bastard. At least Sal is outta the way."

Sally's front garden is almost demolished by the time Jim pulls up. He does a circle turn, facing the way he has come, in case he needs to leave in a hurry. Distancing himself from Andy's activities he watches from his ute, the engine idling, ready for a hasty retreat. There is a growing heap of rose bushes tangled together with black irrigation poly-piping, the buckled remains of wrought iron furniture, a broken bird bath, and lattice work from the shattered white gazebo. Backing up violently, obviously intent on driving the machine around the back to her vegetable garden, Andy clumsily takes out three verandah posts. The ancient, corrugated iron roof of the side verandah slowly collapses.

He swigs on a bottle of rum as he drives the loader across the backyard, swinging the bucket around to demolish the chook shed. Haphazardly scooping up random raised vegetable beds, he drops them in a heap over the fence. He raises the bucket to full height and with a short run-up, drives full force at the tank stand. The poly tank bursts, water cascading across the roof of the carport and onto the driveway. With a second inadvertent but expediently placed thrust, he takes out the rest of the tank stand and collapses the carport.

Jim watches as the loader careers to the shed, Andy jumping out to hysterically fling several old tyres into the bucket followed by a jerrycan of fuel and the gas weed burner. He throws his rifle, a box of ammunition and a spare magazine into the cab and drives erratically back to the house. Along the way the loader's rear ballast box entangles the temporary wire fence restricting cattle access to several rolls of hay. It unravels and trails behind him, its spindly wooden droppers forced into a reluctant juddering dance.

Pulsating clouds of dust explode along the driveway, then mingle to float gently across the paddocks towards town. Rachel leads in her old Holden station wagon, followed by her brothers. Jase and young Dougy, his son, are in Dougy's ute. Nifty is in his truck with the firefighting tank and unit on the back. Tommo trails behind in the ancient fire truck purchased third or fourth-hand a decade ago. It is the back up for the local Bushfire Brigade. The convoy turns one by one into the paddock to park next to each other in a line facing the farmhouse. This way they are able to see and call out to each other.

Upending his rum bottle, Andy drains it in two gulps and hurls it out into the paddock. The loader engine is idling gently as he falls drunkenly out onto the concrete. He heaves the tyres through windows, shattering the glass and staggering backwards from the effort. Mission completed, he yanks back the cap on the jerrycan and splashes petrol clumsily along the timber walls, and through broken windows onto the tyres. When it is empty, he raises it in both hands above his head, and heaves it through the kitchen window. It takes three attempts to ignite the weed burner and he stumbles around the house, setting light to the tyres and the trail of petrol, smashing the remaining intact windows and directing the flame inside.

He turns to stare at his neighbours. In his drunken frenzy, the line of nosy fuckin', interferin' bastards are facing him off, challenging him, their engines running as they wait to run him down. He yells at them incoherently, his voice now overwhelmed by the sudden roaring of flames. Columns of black smoke begin billowing into the sky. Retrieving his rifle from the loader cabin he cowers behind one of the far side rear wheels, eyeing off his combatants, before firing random shots at them. As one they duck down below their dashboards.

The windscreen on the fire truck shatters into a million crystalline fragments. Tommo turns off the engine, grabs at the two-way radio, opens the door, and slides to the ground. He attempts to crawl commando style on his elbows but hampered by his large ungainly gut, instead scurries on his bum around the back, positioning himself to peek out from behind the dual rear wheels.

Rachel, clear-headed and competent in a crisis, is on the phone to the Police.

"I'm at Andy Chester's farm on Preston Road. That is five kilometres south of the South West Highway, left turn just after the Preston bridge." Her windscreen shatters, showering her with pebbles of glass. She cowers further down in the front seat, head under the passenger dashboard. "He is drunk, hysterical, armed, and has set his house on fire." There is another gunshot and she feels a front tyre deflate. "There are two Bush Brigade vehicles and two other farm vehicles, five men and myself present." Another shot and the other front tyre deflates. "He has just shot out my windscreen and two front tyres. You need to get here *now*!." She pauses, listening. "This won't wait until your bloody sergeant gets in." She listens again.

"We *are* waiting and watching. *You need to get here now.!!* she screams, "And send a bloody ambulance!"

Not fifteen minutes later, Andy is distracted by the sound of sirens, and looks to see two police cars leading an ambulance, three more farm utes, a car, a tractor and three young fellas on motorbikes in another dusty convoy hurtling down his driveway. There is a growing line of assorted vehicles backed up along the access road to the farm. The black tyre smoke, seen from kilometres away, has signalled farmers all around who have dropped their morning routines to speed to this flaming emergency, or at least to see what it's all about. Those brave enough venture up to the centre of the calamity, encircle the raging inferno from a safe distance. Heralding their arrival, first one and then the other LP gas cylinders on the side verandah explode.

"He's gonna catch his self on fire!" yells Nifty.

"Ah stupid bastard." Tommo unwinds the truck's fire hose and starts up the petrol motor for the pump. "Hey Jim, give me some cover will ya."

Jim Kessel does a U turn to park his ute in front of Tommo's truck. The hose is pointed not at the house but at the loader and Andy, showering them both in water. Nifty backs in behind Jim and does the same. Andy, overwhelmed by the duel cascades, falls to the ground. He flails helplessly on his back, splattered with water and mud. He is struggling to breathe let alone continue to yell the profanities he's been discharging at his neighbours. Eventually he is able to roll over onto his hands and knees and uses the tread lugs on the loader's rear wheels to lever himself up off the ground. Slipping and sliding beneath the prolonged watery assault, he manages to throw his rifle into the loader cab and climb back in.

*"Watch and wait! Nobody move. Stay in your vehicles."* A young policeman stands beside his car, CB radio in one hand, megaphone in the other.

*"Do not, I repeat, DO NOT leave your vehicles. Stay low and out of sight!"*

A cacophony of voices is immediately launched from the bystanders.

"What's he sayin?'

"Turn your bloody radio on!"

"Stay in ya bloody car!"

"What?"

"What channel is it?"

"Five or thirty five!"

"What?"

"He said ta stay in ya fuckin car. Don't move ya stupid bastard."

"Bloody Five or thirty fuckin' five!"

"What?"

"I haven't got a radio!"

"What?"

"Channel bloody five!"

"Just watch and do what we do."

"Watch out! He's makin' a move."

"Stupid bloody bastard!"

Andy engages the loader gears and charges the most recent line up of vehicles, unhampered by the wire fence still attached to the ballast box and bouncing unhappily behind him. Vehicles scatter. The motorcyclists, their experience in rounding cattle through paddocks making them the most nimble, scoot around to the far side of the dam. They stand, one foot each anchoring them to the ground, the other poised on the footrest, using the hand throttles to rev their engines like panting bulls waiting to charge. One police car races down the driveway to block the gate. There begins a comical choreography as Andy chases his neighbours across and around his house paddock, still trailing the length of wire fence with its dancing wooden stakes.

The young policeman stares in bewilderment as the pantomime unfolds. He can hardly tell them to stay put and risk being assaulted by Andy's loader. The ambulance has retreated to park, engine running, next to the farm shed. Smoke and flames continue to billow into the sky, the remaining intact windows are exploding and the two firehoses have now been redirected futilely towards the house.

Tommo is the first to intervene, yelling into his radio.

"Any of you bastards got a rifle? We need ta shoot out the loader's tyres."

*"Do not, I repeat, DO NOT use your firearms,"* orders the young policeman.

"So whadda ya suggest? We all get in a cosy circle and close in on the stupid bastard?" yells Tommo, shaking his head in disgust.

Tom Kessel turns off his motor, heaves himself out of his seat and rolls his weight around to the passenger door where he reaches behind the seat. He's too old for this bullshit. These young'uns need some real leadership. He pulls out his rifle, retrieves the bolt and magazine from the glove box and clicks them competently into place. Using the side gates on the ute's tray as a gun rest, he waits for Andy to falter in his rampage, and places three shots each into the rear wheels. Water spurts out of each hole. It will take several minutes of driving haphazardly on them before they have deflated sufficiently to disable the loader.

With rifle in hand, Andy clambers down and stumbles drunkenly to the farm shed, where he scrambles for more ammunition and cowers behind a stack of hay. His neighbours drive their vehicles to either side of the shed, out of firing range. They begin tentatively congregating together, second-guessing what has happened, what is going on, and where it is all likely to end. A couple of the more courageous, or fool-hardy ones, creep stealthily to the corners of the shed to peep quickly in Andy's direction, unable to see him, but gauging his whereabouts from his spasmodic rifle shots.

The police car remains in place at the farm gate blocking access from the growing number of voyeurs arriving to investigate the spectacle. The young policeman with the megaphone, and his partner, now with the CB radio, park their car sideways about twenty metres in front of the shed. They remove themselves to the car's rear side, where they can maintain a clear and protected view of their assailant. Their watch-and-wait protocol is reinstated.

* * *

Friday lunchtime.

There are four messages when Brian thinks to check his phone. He, Milton and Sally have returned from a long bare-foot beach walk. At Sally's behest, they have talked about anything but Andy. Brian explained his options for taking the position in Broome, full-time or fly in, fly out; two weeks on, one week off; both with accommodation provided. He teased Milton with potential hospitality management work for him at one of the five-star resorts. At least one return flight to the city available each day, Grannie's house their city accommodation. Would he consider a sea change?

Much of the conversation explored Sally's options for her immediate future, perhaps living with them in Grannie's house, Milton suggesting the possibility of part-time shifts in the gift shop of the Ambassador International Hotel. She understands their need to have her resettled and safe, but has no wish to be anywhere other than the shack and the beach, to consider anything or anywhere beyond the now. She needs this retreat. She needs to heal. This separation, the silence, and the sea, are soothing her soul.

"Sorry Sal," says Brian, mobile phone in hand as he re-joins them on the shack verandah. "There were messages from the Police for me to call them. There has been an incident with Andy." He hesitates, not sure how to tell her what has happened. Oh just do it.

"Andy has burned the farmhouse down. He has barri-caded himself in the shed and is shooting at the Police. It seems he is very drunk, very angry, and they are biding their time until he gives in or runs out of ammunition... I'm sorry. You really don't need this."

"Were they informing us or requesting that we do some-thing?" Sally is perfectly composed, almost business-like.

"Initially informing me... us. They wanted to know where you are, if you are safe. Then what we know about what might have set him off."

"So what did you tell them? I really don't want anyone to know where I am. I don't want people questioning me, or visiting me. I'm happy as I am." Brian is both surprised and encouraged by her candid affirmative response.

"I told them that you have left Andy, and that he was served with your custody and business termination affida-vits yesterday. I also told them you are with Millie and me, and that we are currently staying with friends. They seemed okay with all that, and will keep us informed."

"Did they ask to speak to me?

"They suggested that it would be helpful if you could speak to them. I told them it would be most *unhelpful* to you, unless it is absolutely necessary. I also told them you have disconnected your mobile phone. They didn't need to know that you now have a new one."

Sally grins. "Thank you." She releases her plaited hair and shakes it free, running her fingers comb like through it and shaking her head in a semicircular motion. "I'm really not surprised. Though I am relieved he's contained his violent response to the farm."

"Aren't you concerned about the house?" asks Milton.

She thinks for a moment before replying. "No... If I'm honest, I'm relieved. It's final. It's finished. For too long it has held too many ghosts. The boys brought light and laughter to it when they were young, but since they have been away at school..." She trails off and reconsiders what she is thinking, what she is feeling, what she wishes to say. "I've already let it go, so there's nothing lost that I will mourn. There are things the boys will have lost that might cause them some fleeting disappointments perhaps. But they'll get over it."

"So what do you want to do now?" asks Brian. "The Police will contact us when the situation has been resolved. One way or another." He is feeling very protective towards her. She has been in such a great place. While he and Milton have expected Andy to behave irrationally, this has surprised them both. It seems the man has imploded. He especially does not want Sally to be wounded by it in any way.

"I want Wal to join us, to sit around a campfire, to eat good food, to have a few drinks, and just have a bloody good time." She laughs. They laugh in both surprise and approval with her.

"Well I'm always up for a party." says Milton. "You go get Wal. Brian you start the fire. Leave the food and drinkies to me"

\* \* \*

They have all finished eating and are enjoying a billy tea when Brian's mobile phone rings. He walks away and takes the call on the shack verandah, where he is less likely to be overheard. Milton and Sally are looking at each other in silent expectation, resignation even. Walter, sensing this immediate change in mood, looks enquiringly at them both. Sally knows she needs to tell him. It was inevitable that he would have to know. She has been so enjoying their frivolous distractions. But now it's time.

"Andy burned the farmhouse down this morning. He has been barricaded in the shed, shooting at the Police. That will be them informing us what has happened. Hopefully it has been resolved without anyone getting hurt."

"Oh Sal. I'm sorry. This must be hard for you." He looks to Milton. "For all of you. And we've just been having the best time. I never realised. I'm so sorry."

"It's alright," smiles Sally. "We *have* been having a wonderful time. Thank you. It was what I asked of Brian and Millie." She leans to Milton who is sitting next to her and places her hand on his arm. "Millie, you and Brian, and you too Wal, have been so kind. You have been my rocks, and my distractions." She hesitates. "Since letting go, *really letting* go, I feel like I have no fight left in me." She looks towards the shack where Brian seems to be listening more than he is talking. "I just want it to end... It's been so long... I'm tired. I'm so tired of it all."

Brian returns.

"Andy is in custody. He has been sectioned and is under guard in the psychiatric ward at the hospital."

"Did he surrender?" asks Milton.

"Well yes and no. It seems he kept everyone at bay for several hours and then his neighbour, Jim Kessel....."

"I know Jim," says Sally.

"Jim was first there this morning. He went home when the police kicked everyone off the property, but he'd been listening to Andy firing shots; could hear him from his farm. Apparently it got to him and he drove back, convinced the Police he could talk Andy round. He ignored the Police's instructions about caution, just walked straight up to Andy and said, 'Stop being a bloody idiot and hand over the bloody gun.' And he did." Sally laughs. Milton and Walter smile, unsure whether to join her.

"He took the gun off Andy, gave it to the police then told Andy 'to get his arse out of there and into the police car'. Apparently Andy was blubbering like a big kid and just walked out."

"So what will happen now?" asks Milton. "Are you OK Sal love?" She smiles and nods.

"He will be detained up to three days pending psychiatric assessment." Brian replies. "Though this could be delayed by the weekend. Depending on that assessment, he'll likely be sent to the Graylands Mental Hospital. When I told the Police that Andy doesn't own the farm, they said that would add to their case for charging him with arson. He'll be held on remand after he's released from Graylands. Assuming he is released that is."

Sally lets out a heavy sigh. "He has nowhere to live now anyway. No family. Well no immediate family other than me and the boys. I can't imagine any of his cousins will want to take him in."

"The Police did say that as you're still legally his next of kin, they and the psychiatric assessment team will be wanting to talk to you." says Brian. "Sorry Sal. But I did manage to get them to agree to wait until Monday. I assured them that you will contact them by midday then. That gives you time to meet with Wal's niece if that can be arranged."

"It can. It will." says Walter.

Milton stands behind Sally and rests a hand on each of her shoulders. She leans her head to one side resting it against his arm. She has nothing to say. They all sit in silence, looking into the campfire coals. The party is over.

# Chapter 11

Six months later

"You'll never guess who I found." Brian steps onto the deck of the bungalow he shares with Sally at Cable Beach in Broome. She looks up from where she is luxuriating in a rattan armchair, bare feet resting on the matching coffee table. Her hair is cropped and she is wearing a batik sarong over her bathers. A beaming Walter steps up and waits to greet her. She places her book face down on the table and slowly stands, smiling as she moves into his silent embrace. They stand holding each other for a full minute before stepping apart, eyes connecting and celebrating this meeting.

"You look well." says Walter.

"I am," replies Sally. "And you?"

"Oh I am well. Very well. And happy." He grins. "And you?"

"I am happy. Very happy." They both laugh and hug each other again.

"Look I've gotta go." says Brian. "Management meeting in ten minutes. I'll be finished by six. Can we get together for dinner after then?"

"Absolutely." replies Walter. "Sal, it is so good to see you." He turns to Brian. "It is so good to see you both. I'd heard you had taken up this job offer. I hoped I might see you. I didn't imagine you would be here as well Sal." He pulls up a chair, sits on its edge and leans over to take her hand in both of his. They beam at each other. He releases her and sits back, waiting for her to speak. She doesn't. Brian leaves.

"So... How long have you been here? What are you doing? Are you planning to stay long? Are you working?"

She bursts out laughing. "Wal, I've never heard you ask so many questions? Which one do you want me to answer first?" She laughs again.

"Oh any," he too laughs.

"Brian took the fly-in, fly-out option at the beginning of December. He wanted to still have time for me and the boys until everything was sorted, so he's only been full-time since the beginning of March, three weeks now. He intends to take long weekends back in Perth with Millie, and vice versa. They will still manage to have quality time together.

"I came back with him at the start of this new contract. I was at Grannies house until then." She sits back into her chair, crossing her legs and readjusting her sarong. "I'm staying for at least another three weeks, till after Easter. Millie is bringing the boys up for the school holidays. He has to get back but we'll all have a week together. The boys will fly back a week later." She laughs. "Millie's their city mum for the time being, and just loving it. I've said I'll fly back with them. Though I so love it here. It's quiet, and private. And the ocean..... I take long morning walks along the beach and go for a swim, when the tide is in."

They sit smiling at each other.

"Let me make you a coffee." She says, standing and moving towards the doorway. "We have a proper machine here."

"That'd be nice. Strong white with two sugars. Actually, I'd love a cappuccino if your machine is up to it." He stretches out his long legs, flipping his sandals one by one onto the deck. He is dressed in comfortably baggy faded farm shorts and an equally faded button up cotton check shirt. Sally returns with two steaming mugs and a plate of cheese and savoury biscuits.

"We don't eat sweet biscuits or cake, I'm sorry."

"The coffee will be just fine. " says Walter and takes a sip, wiping the froth from his upper lip. "You're looking really good Sal. Your hair..... it suits you." He is beaming at her.

"So what brings *you* to Broome?" she asks. "Did you fly or drive? Are you here for work or a holiday? Are Joey or any of the family with you?"

He laughs, a rich, relaxed belly laugh. "So who's asking all the questions now?....... I drove. Been here three days. Well, three nights. I got in just before dark. Joey's getting married. That distraction in the city when he dropped me off at the shacks?" He pauses, raising his eyebrows in a be-mused frown. "They're having a small family wedding here this weekend. Well, Friday evening. Day after tomorrow." He takes a long swallow of his coffee.

"Wow." says Sally. "The first of your kids to be married. You'll be a grandad before you know it."

"Nah. Joey and Anita, that's his fiancée. They want to spend some time working in the Kimberley. She's done jillaroo work up here before. But she graduated from Curtin Uni with a degree in Environmental Science last year and hopes to get work in one of the National Parks. They're just roadhouse hopping for a few months to get a feel for the top end and see if this is where they want to be."

"Roadhouse hopping?"

"A mate of Joey's told him there's always casual work at roadhouses, food and accommodation provided and especially for couples, 'cos that makes accommodation easier. They've already contacted a few and have work lined up well into the dry season. Till next October if they want it. First stop Willare Bridge."

"I take it they're here already?"

"Yes. We drove in convoy with Anita's Mum and Dad. They're using this as stage one of a trip across the Kimberley to Darwin and then down through the centre. The usual, Bungles, Kakadu, Uluru, Coober Pedy, Adelaide and back across to W.A."

"And you?"

" I've an old friend managing Bonney Downes Station. I'm going to stay with him for a few weeks. Apart from the odd few days at the shacks, I haven't had a proper holiday; well extended time right away from the farm, since.... Oh before Kath got sick. We never.... Well it just didn't happen. I'm ready now." He smiles a weary smile. "You didn't say. Are you working?"

"No. Not ready yet. I'm still not up to being with or around people. Not ready to answer all their questions. People usually want to know your life story. I just don't want to talk about mine. Better nothing, no story, than lies or evasions." She looks at Walter and smiles. "Your questions are fine. You already know most of my life story. And anyway, I have absolutely no idea what I want to do."

There is a companionable silence between them. Walter has finished his coffee. Sally is still sipping on hers. Each is thinking of the other, so thrilled to be together again, to see each is well and happy. They smile together, eyes mirroring their mutual joy. They had only known each other those seven days. Walter had left the shacks shortly after Brian and Sally, as they made their way back to the city. Needing to consult with Jennifer before talking with the Police and psychiatrist, she and Brian had agreed that she should do so in person.

They are remembering their last goodbye. Walter had assured her that all would be well. They had exchanged phone numbers and he had asked her to promise to phone him if she needed him, for anything. She promised she would. Both knew that she wouldn't. They had held each other a long time in silent embrace, until Sally whispered into his chest.

"Wal..... Thank you. I..... I...... Thank you."

He had rested his lips against her hair and whispered, "You are welcome. It has been my pleasure. Go well my Sal."

Conversation at a standstill, a hesitant cloud floating between them, Walter slides his feet back into his sandals and stands politely to leave. Sally stands as if readying herself to accompany him back to his car. They both hesitate.

"I don't have to be anywhere," he says with a grin.

"I don't want you to go," she replies. He returns to his chair, sits, and waves her back into to hers.

"Will you stay for lunch? I can phone Brian and have him organise for something to be sent over. I don't want to go anywhere. Be anywhere," she smiles. "I just want to sit here... with you."

He leans forward and places a square of cheese onto a biscuit. "I'd love another coffee and a glass of water." There is so much to say. Neither knows where to start. Coffee, it's making and drinking, is the transitional distraction they both need. Sally leans over to reclaim his mug, standing as she picks up her own. She turns to say something, changes her mind, her leg brushing his as she moves past.

They sit sipping on their coffees. Who will start the ball rolling? Walter can see she is in a good place, despite her understandable reluctance to engage with people. He wants to ask how her journey has been since they last saw each other. He is surprised at how much he cares; unsettled even; these emerging emotions expanding since he first saw her and held her again.

Sally wants to tell him what has happened with her and the boys, with Brian and Millie. He was the catalyst to so much of her letting go, enabling her journey towards healing. She wants to explain why she never phoned, to share with him how far she has travelled through her sessions with Stanley. She too is shocked by her surge of feelings at seeing him, being with him. She has thought of him often these past months. She knows how lucky she was to meet him and have him there when she most needed him. But not once had she considered contacting him.

"You must be wondering what has happened since you saw me last," she finally says. "A lot of doors have closed,...... thankfully."

"I saw that Andy pleaded guilty to the arson charges, and that he's on remand waiting on the Supreme Court hearing."

"Yes."

"Is that door closed? asks Walter.

"Emotionally, financially, legally; yes. I might have to attend the court hearing. And I can't start divorce proceedings until we've been separated for twelve months. I've officially, legally, relinquished my status as his next of kin. He agreed to the accountant being Power of Attorney. He had no choice really." Walter nods.

"You know how it is on a farm. Arranging for the last of the crops to be harvested, the cattle sold off, insurances cancelled, finances settled. The machinery and equipment were auctioned. The business lease on the farm paid out and terminated." Walter leans forward to replace his coffee cup with the glass of water.

"Yes," he says. "You've done well Sal. I mean, you could have just walked away. But then that's just so not who you are." He pauses to take a swallow of water. "So what's happening now? You haven't been back?"

"No. There's padlocks on the gates, nothing happening.... for the time being. I've engaged someone to arrange for a new lease agreement with the right client, in my role as the boys' trustee. Jennifer has helped with that. She's been amazing. She is so good at her job."

"Indeed she is," smiles Walter.

"And given that Andy is no longer in a position to work the farm, the accountant, in his capacity as Power of Attorney and discussions with Jennifer, has transferred half of the business capital and the proceeds of the sales and auctions to me. Apparently he informed Andy beforehand and it seems there was no resistance. I mean, given his charge of arson, it was possible his assets would be frozen, if not confiscated anyway."

"Did you have to see him? See Andy?"

"Brian and I visited him in Graylands Mental Hospital. The psychiatrist who was case managing him asked us to. He, Andy, was obviously sedated. But even so, he is broken, completely broken. He couldn't make eye contact. Didn't speak. Ignored the psychiatrist and social worker."

"How was that for you Sal? It can't have been easy."

"You know, after all those years of managing my emotions with him, holding onto my power in not...in never reacting to him, to his moods, to his spoken and unspoken challenges, his attempts at bullying, it was easy. It was the end.... It was the end I'd always been working towards. The end I've been waiting for. So it was an enormous relief and... and a release."

"Oh Sal. So long, living like that, locked in that relationship. For the very best of reasons as you've told me. But it must have been like a prison sentence."

"Not in the beginning. When I first moved in, I was so intent on being in charge of my own life. With my advancing pregnancy, I had an enormous belly, I.... It was the reminder of Andy's transgression, his violating of me," She is unable to say the word rape. "It was in his face, every day. And that's where I wanted it to be. I think perhaps at first, he *was* ashamed." She ruminates on this a while before continuing. "Though not once did he speak of it, apologise, or try to make amends. He was sullen and silent, absenting himself from the house most of the time. In the shed, out in the paddocks; and the pub. That was the beginning of his daily visits to the pub."

"And Margaret? Your mother-in-law?"

"Well it was in her face too. What her son had done. And unspoken between us, was the knowledge that she had seen him doing it and did nothing, said nothing,... her *own* cowardice. Once we were married she never discussed it. The conditions, the boundaries, had been set. She had agreed to them. It was too late for her to reconsider or haggle over them. And she was never going to. That was the implied agreement for me to remain silent on what Andy had done." She is thinking about Margaret, there relationship, how it began, how it changed, how it ended.

"She *was* helpful in supporting my pregnancy. It was quite uncomfortable towards the end, and of course she was a nurse. ... And I admit, she was also a great support when the boys were babies. But she was working full time until she had her first stroke, shortly after they turned eight. So I had the house to myself most of the time. I made it mine. I made it the home I wanted for my babies, my boys." She smiles. "They, Andy and Margaret, weren't comfortable at first, with the changes I was making to what had always been *their* home. I didn't care. I just ignored any protests. There weren't any from Andy. And it was actually a great improvement.

"I held the power. I had to,... for the boys,... for the three of us. If I'm honest, truly honest with myself, as Stanley has helped me to be, I *was* motivated by a sense of revenge, *not* just forcing them to take responsibility. But there was no anger, no rage, no resentment. Not from me or from them. It was a business arrangement and I was in control. He... They owed me."

"But what about the boys? How did they cope with the tensions in the household? Kids can really pick up on what's going on, even if they don't understand it. Adults' anxieties, their anger or rages, even the silences. If a parent is grieving, or sulking or detached." Walter is more than curious. He is discovering just how remarkable this younger woman is, and has been. He is also remembering, his own challenges, his own children. Some of the difficult times.

"They *were* frightened of him when they were very small, before they went to school, but only when he had his tantrums. And those were always about his own frustrations with work. You know, machinery breakdowns, irrigation pipes bursting or leaking, cows calving or dying. They were never about me or directed towards me . Well not then. I made sure that his domestic needs were met, predicting what he would be needing, wanting, so that he had no reason to argue with me. I treated it as a job. I ensured he had no legitimate domestic or business grounds for complaint. I held the power." She takes a long drink of water.

"I made sure the boys knew their father was not angry with *them*. I made sure their home was a happy place, a safe place. And when it wasn't, I took them away. A picnic, a play date with school friends, a few days in the city with Uncle Brian and Aunty Milly." She smiles. "They loved that. Especially as they got older and could go sailing. And I would tell Andy, like you would a child, when his behaviour towards me or in front of the boys was inappropriate or unacceptable. To take it elsewhere. You know, an adult version of 'Your behaviour is unacceptable. Go to your room.'" They both laugh.

Now immersed in these memories, she continues. "Early on Margaret sometimes attempted to intervene, to make excuses for him, to counter *my* management and manipulations. I just reminded her that my marriage to her son was a business arrangement, to which she, and he, had agreed. And that I would not be putting up with his juvenile behaviours nor her attempted interventions on his behalf." She grins.

"Ho Sal," laughs Walter; "You *were* a feisty one. Well done you!"

"I couldn't have done it," she says, "learned how to manage my emotions, be assertive and fearless, without Stanley.

I just can't imagine what I would have done without him, his support, his wisdom, his mentoring."

"So when did Andy change? I mean it has been obvious from Brian's descriptions that he really did qualify for the title of Arsehole."

"A year or so after Margaret had her strokes. She had lost much of her speech, found it really taxing to communicate with him. He had no patience with her. So she was less able to manage him. And my time was taken up more in caring for her. That impacted on my domestic routines. He would be pissed off by the interruptions caused by her care needs. And of course after she died.... my health had begun to weaken. I was so tired all the time. It wasn't until I had those blood transfusions and my surgery that I realised just how seriously depleted I had become. Thankfully the boys were at boarding school by then.

"But you know, seeing Andy that last time, with everything that has happened, the house gone, his farm, his future finished, I almost felt sorry for him. He has nothing. Absolutely nothing.... Nobody. He knows he's facing a significant gaol sentence, and will likely have to pay compensation to the boys for the house, the infrastructure losses on the farm. I told him he is not to make any direct contact with me or the boys, *ever*. He's on his own. And he knows it. That door is closed."

"And the boys? Yes it's over, but with so much loss and drama. It can't have been easy for them either."

"I've learned, they have shown me, that we seriously underestimate the intelligence and resilience of our children. They were amazing. We, well Brian, Millie and I, took them out of school for a week, to have family time; going sailing, to the movies, ten pin bowling. Just being together and available to answer their questions...... They didn't have many. They now know that they share ownership of the farm. They accept that their father is mentally ill." She pauses and smiles. "You know, they actually said to us, 'We've always known that Dad was crazy. Didn't you?'" She looks into her coffee mug before returning her focus to Walter.

"Any plans? For yourself?" he asks as he drains his water glass and places it on the table.

"Intentions. But no plans. Like I said, Stanley has been amazing, as always. He visited me at Grannies house, just before Christmas; and I have had some long talks with him on the phone. He is such a wise and gentle human being." She smiles, their mutual understanding of her needs, and Stanley's capacity to counsel her, sitting unsaid between them.

"The boys finish school at the end of this year. They're happy to continue boarding and spending their holidays with Millie and me at Grannies house. I've always enjoyed the city for a visit, and it was the perfect place to be after..... well after everything. But I don't want to live there. I find it so confronting; the noise, the traffic, the pace. It's almost overwhelming. And suburbia is just too ordered; all those manicured lawns and driveways. Too contrived, claustrophobic. I guess I'm a country girl through and through."

"Yep. I can relate to that," says Walter. "It's why I love the shacks. In fact the whole family always has. There's room for everyone, even if the kids end up swagging it on the verandahs."

"Brian and Millie have been just fabulous," continues Sally. "They would have me live with them for as long as I want. But I don't want to piggyback my life on their's. They and their friends are lots of fun, lots of laughs, but I don't fit. Like I never felt I fitted in the town life beyond the farm. It was fine being a part of organisations while the boys were little and at school; involved in the community life that supported their growing up years; but after they left......that was it really. My identity has just been wife and mother. Otherwise, I don't really know who I am, or might be."

"Not interested in nursing? Study?" asks Walter.

"Not now. Not after Margaret. Stanley has always asked me, what gives me pleasure? What do I enjoy doing for myself, not just for other people?" She sighs. "Raising the boys, working the farm business, finding enjoyable things to do within the constraints imposed on me; or as he has long reminded me, the constraints I imposed on myself. I have no constraints now. None. The boys are fine. They have Brian and Millie. Just like they always have, but more so now they're older. I know I don't need to worry about them. So now that I have endless choices, I just don't know what I want to do....... Or who I want to be." She laughs. "Stanley has suggested I just be, and to stop trying. Perhaps then the real me will just evolve and surprise me."

"So what *do* you enjoy doing Sal. What has given you pleasure.?"

"Oh I've always enjoyed being creative. Loved cooking. Enjoyed sewing, handicrafts, growing my own organic vegetables, my chooks, filling my pantry with pickles and jams and bottled fruits. But I'm thinking now that was more about what I believed I was *meant* to be doing. Feeling good about myself by trying to be perfect at everything I did." She grins. "You could say I was a bit up myself really." She laughs. Walter laughs with her.

She has phoned Brian and lunch arrives. They immerse themselves in the delights and delicacies collated for them, and share a bottle of chilled white wine. Walter entertains her with some of the challenges and experiences of travelling for four days with his son, his prospective daughter-in-law and her parents. Anita's Mum was a bit of a control freak, wanting to organise everyone, when and where they ate, where they stayed, what time they needed to leave, all the while being overtly friendly and helpful, just micromanaging everyone, everything.

Walter laughs. "She was most concerned that I was travelling alone, and that I didn't have a wife, a woman, to wash my underpants for me. She offered to wash mine with hers and her poor long suffering husband's, like they couldn't sit in a suitcase and just had to be washed every day for heaven's sake. I was going to assure her that I had packed enough to last me the trip, and also that I was more than capable of doing my own laundry. I've been doing it for years. But I settled on telling her that I never wear any. That shut her up." They both laugh exuberantly.

"Oh Sal, I do enjoy being with you."

"Me too," she replies.

"We are so easy together. Good for each other."

"We are." She grins and nods in agreement.

"And I am so pleased to see you well, and happy, after all you've been through." He pauses. "I want to spend some time with you. Without any distractions." She considers this, but just fleetingly. She is a free agent. The boys and Millie not arriving for another week.

"I'd love that Wal. I've missed you. And I never phoned you. I... I did think about you. A lot. I just needed to....

"Hey. No explanations. I wasn't expecting you to. I told you. I am here if ever you need me. Even come stay with me on the farm if it suits, and you want to get away. Anyway; I have family flying up for the weekend, for this wedding. But everyone is leaving Monday. I've no time constraints. Don't have to be at Bonney Downes until I get there." He hesitates. "Just so we're clear. No expectations. No promises. I'm not looking for a relationship. I just want us to have some uninterrupted time together. I'm not sure either of us is ready for anything other than friendship. But I feel like we have been friends forever."

"Always on the same page, you and I," she says with a smile. "And you're right. I'm not looking for... I don't want a relationship." They rest in agreement, comfortably acknowledging this mutual need and intention.

Sally speaks. "But I *do* want us to enjoy some holiday time together. I am so comfortable with you Wal. I can be *me* with you. Whoever me is. She, me, is still becoming."

"So how do we go about this? What will work for you?"

"If only we could have the shacks up here. Their simplicity, no people." She says. "Our individual spaces but close enough to be together when we want to. No obligations, privacy, silence, the ocean." She smiles, remembering.

"Are you happy to leave it with me?"

"Always."

"Tell you what. How about I just collect you from here at two 'o'clock Monday. Surprise destination. Three nights. Back for the afternoon plane when Milton and the boys arrive."

"Perfect." She stands and collects their plates and the leftovers. "Tea or coffee? Or water?"

"A strong cup of tea I reckon. Milk, two sugars. Can I help?"

"Nope," she replies and scuttles inside.

She places his steaming mug of tea before him and rests her tall glass of mineral water on the table. "How old are your kids Wal?"

"Joey is twenty-four. No, twenty-five. Soon. The week after Easter. Matty is twenty-two. We've left him in charge of the farm. Linda would have been twenty. We lost her when she was five. She drowned. In the dam. Nobody's fault. It just happened."

"Oh Wal, I'm so sorry. I didn't know."

"No. Well. It was a long time ago. Kath never got over it. You don't really. But let's not dwell on that. I want to know more about your boys. Do *they* have any plans?"

She is still reeling from Walter's reference to his daughter. She almost wishes she hadn't asked him about his kids. But are her feelings, is her regret, more about her own woundedness than his? There had been times when she had wished for a daughter, but pushed those thoughts, any thoughts of more children, a loving relationship, aside.

"They both want to go to Uni. Matt is interested in architecture. Benjie is undecided. He's quite taken with marine biology, or environmental science. I'm not sure. But anyway, whatever they want to do, they have the means to get them started. In fact, support them well on their way."

"That just leaves you Sal". He leans back in his chair and speaks slowly, gently. "What you *want* to do, what is *meant* for you, will find you when you're ready. Don't rush. Be kind to yourself. It's *your* time now."

"I'm beginning to accept that it is." She sighs and smiles. "For so long my choices, my whole focus, was on the boys;

their wellbeing, my fears for their futures, my fears for them knowing and believing in themselves. It was obsessive. It's like my mission has been to compensate for the manner of their conception. They don't know how and why I married their father. I hope they never ask. I'd prefer not to have to lie to them, but I suspect I will." He knows she has more to say. His heart is open. He hopes she can feel it so.

"I've been able to tell Brian and Millie how it happened. They accepted the facts; accepted my choices..... They haven't pushed me for explanations. Stanley helped me from the very beginning to see, to believe, that Matt and Benjie were in fact a gift. Unintended, unwanted, but a gift. And they have been. They have been my world." Again she hesitates, considering what she is trying to say. "Being pregnant, so young, just out of the blue. Having to make enormous, life-changing choices. So many responsibilities and challenges just dropped on me. I believe I've met them. I'm not proud of all the choices I made. But my boys have brought me so much joy. And I'm proud of the young men they are growing to be."

"And so you should be. You are an amazing woman.." He hesitates. Is this the right time? He is about to challenge her. She reminds him so much of his Kath. Her strengths and her vulnerabilities. Her self-protective determination. Her past paralysing her passage to her future. He wants to help her move on. He believes she is ready.

"One day Sal you *will* tell the boys how they were conceived." She is stunned.

"They might never ever ask how you came to be with their father. But I'm guessing they've wondered; that they've already talked about it between themselves. And just like

Brian and Millie, caring for you so much, they don't want to shame or distress you."

He sees her posture stiffen. Is she defensive or just uneasy?

" One day you will tell them the truth. It is *their truth too* you know." She is about to protest. He keeps going.

"No more secrets," he says gently. "You *can't* keep on living that lie if you want to move on. Do this for *yourself.* Do it for *them.*" She shifts uncomfortably in her chair. She has never considered sharing *this* truth with her boys. Her life's mission has been to keep it *from* them, to compensate for it. To create a stable life for them, encourage their joint and individual interests and endeavours, ensuring their connections to family and community. And most of all, establishing a strong and trusting relationship with them; never manipulating, intent on inspiring and nurturing their confidence, their independence and personal responsibility. The very opposite to the immaturity and narcissism of their father.

He continues, "You can explain their conception without telling them exactly what happened. They need to know that your marriage was not normal. One of the first things you said to me was *'Ours was not a normal marriage.'* Well your boys need to know that too." She wants to respond but doesn't know what to say. And she doesn't want to defend herself. Not with Wal!

"The boys should be told that it was a business arrangement. They need to know that their mother did *not* have an intimate relationship with their father. They need to know what sits at the heart of your choices. The choices you made for *them.*"

He leans forward and takes her hand. "I am speaking to you as a man, knowing how your sons will look to you, and your example, when they reach manhood; when they are considering an intimate relationship for themselves. I'm speaking as a son and as a father. And I'm speaking as the husband to a woman who was betrayed and wounded, just as you have been. Your boys need to know the wonderful woman, the committed loving mother that you *are*. Not just the mother that *you* would have them see; that you want them to *believe* you are. You owe them that."

She feels tears welling in her eyes and looks away. She is not hurt. She is not angry. With all that Stanley has helped her to see, to feel, and to know about herself, he never managed to touch this place in her. Walter knows he has pushed a boundary. He knows he has opened a window to Sal's deep self, a place she has avoided. He knows from his life with Kath, that for her to find true peace and freedom she needs another to shine their light and especially their love on this wound.

"Sal, you know I care for you very much. You remind me so much of my Kath. You're not at all like her, other than carrying a deep hurt. But the truth you and I share together is similar to what Kath and I had. Yes we were husband and wife, lovers, parents of our three children, but first we were friends. Always we were friends. Always truthful and trusting with each other. That too is a gift. Our gift."

She remains silent, and finds she has to wipe a tear from each eye before they roll down her cheeks. She looks away, towards the tropical garden surrounding her bungalow, seeing none of it. Walter now rests with this silence. He is looking at her with humility and compassion. She is unable to return his gaze. She stands and walks to the edge of the deck, thinking, feeling, composing herself. This time she sees the lush ferns and greenery surrounding her. They ground her. Walter waits. Eventually, she turns to him and speaks.

"I know what you're saying and why. Thank you. I want to think about it. Can you give me a few minutes?" He stands to leave.

"Don't go. Please don't go. I just want time to think over what you just said, to process it." She walks to the other end of the deck, facing away from him, standing still and looking out towards the ocean. Her fingers are entwined in front of her chest, thumbs absent-mindedly rubbing together. This is not the response he expected, but then he doesn't know *what* he expected. He is aware of her long slow deep breathing and unconsciously begins to match it with his own. At last, she turns to face him.

"Wal, you are my friend, as is Stanley. You have both been so good, so kind to me. Accepting, never judging. Caring, never cajoling. It's ironic really that the two people who have most supported me, more than anyone in the world. ...who see me and show me myself, are men." She hesitates again, thinking, clarifying her thoughts; clarifying her feelings.

"I love you both. And I know you both love me. I'd like you to meet each other, with me,..... some time. I know you would *so* get on." She returns to sit next to him and places a hand on his.

"You are so right. My boys *do* need to know the truth. ... They *do* need to know that their parent's relationship, their marriage, was a sham. Brian and Millie have shown them what a strong loving partnership is; been the male role models they needed." She retrieves her hand and sits back in her chair. "Thank you. I needed your truth." She smiles, "Again."

She is once more staring at, but not seeing, the sub-tropical gardens surrounding them. Walter rests comfortably with her continuing contemplation, knowing she wants him there. His presence anchors her as she meanders through her memories, her mindfulness; mulling over what has been said. He has just supplied the last pieces to her emotional jigsaw. It has been years in the making, as she and Stanley dealt with her challenges, her choices and soul searching truths; bringing clarity and understanding, priorities and possibilities to the evolving tapestry of her life. Her renewed health, her intuitive choice to just not get off that bus, her timely meeting with Walter, all combined to create the catalyst allowing her to liberate her secret, unmasking her marriage and allowing it to implode. And ultimately, releasing Andy to descend into the depths of his own dysfunctional destiny. It is, indeed, finished.

Walter has taken himself quietly into the kitchen and returns with two mugs of strong sweet tea. He hands one to Sal, gently bursting her bubble and bringing her back to the moment. She takes it and smiles her appreciation, quietly drinking most of it before turning to him and speaking.

"Wal, there is something I want to ask you. Something I have been thinking about since I've been on holiday here in Broome....... I didn't know you would be here. But now that you are....... I am asking you as my friend. I know too, that if you can't do this, you'll tell me. And you won't be embarrassed or humiliated. We'll still be friends. We'll always be friends."

He doesn't know what to say. He waits, bewildered, looking into her eyes as she looks with complete trust and her raw truth, into his. He has no idea where this is going. She has recovered and returned to her warm, comfortable and confident self. There is now a hint of playfulness in her demeanour. He is relieved and bemusedly intrigued.

"You are the right person; this feels like the right time, and could be the right place. I trust you. Remember?"

"I do." He smiles at the memory. He smiles his confirmation back to her.

"I'm ready," she says.

"So..." he grins. "Friendship with benefits?" She nods and grins back. He stands.

"Come walk with me Sal. And take my hand."

# About the author

Photo: Patricia May family collection

Patricia has lived three lives. The conventional one she was born into and which informs this, her first novel. It is set in a small conservative country town in South Western Australia, similar to where she grew up. From there, she realised her romantic teenage dream of becoming a secondary school teacher and marrying her farmer.

Her second life, meandering intuitively around Central Australia and the East Kimberley, was filled with adventures, challenges, people and places, working with and for remote Indigenous communities and organisations. It was in the middle of nowhere, aka the middle of everywhere, that she met her second husband, who has been her partner in life, professional colleague and travelling companion ever since.

Currently living between Alice Springs and Tasmania, she is happily immersed in her third life of indulgent geriatric eccentricity. She is passionately concerned about the state of our planet and the declining health of its population. These inspire her research into Environmental Sustainability, Regenerative Farming and especially the role of real foods in an Ancestral Diet in supporting physical and mental health and reversing chronic disease. Her second novel will entwine this knowledge with many of the cross-cultural lessons and experiences that have inspired her meaning-of-life reflections and professional redirection to creative writing.